"I've got to save the Berlin Heart."

With a sharp crack, the window fractured and pulled loose. Paul shielded Maggie's body with his.

It could not be true that she was sitting in a crashing plane and the device that would save her father's life was going down with it. Not now, not when she had a chance to fix things.

She peeked behind her at Paul. He had his eyes closed, his lips moving.

He was praying to a God she used to know, a God that let little children die in pain and adults live in agony.

She wished in that moment she still had someone to pray to, to help her with the fear that choked the breath out of her.

"Paul, are we going to die?"

He pushed his hand through the gap between the chairs and squeezed her hand. "We'll make it."

She was grateful for the lie.

Books by Dana Mentink

Love Inspired Suspense

Killer Cargo
Flashover
Race to Rescue
Endless Night
Betrayal in the Badlands
Turbulence

DANA MENTINK

lives in California with her family. Dana and her husband met doing a dinner theater production of *The Velveteen Rabbit*. In college, she competed in national speech and debate tournaments. Besides writing novels, Dana taste-tests for the National Food Lab and freelances for a local newspaper. In addition to her work with Steeple Hill Books, she writes cozy mysteries for Barbour Books. Dana loves feedback from her readers. Contact her at www.danamentink.com.

TURBULENCE
DANA MENTINK

Steeple
Hill®

Published by Steeple Hill Books™

STEEPLE HILL BOOKS

Steeple
Hill®

Recycling programs
for this product may
not exist in your area.

ISBN-13: 978-0-373-44430-4

TURBULENCE

Do not let kindness and truth leave you;
Bind them around your neck,
Write them on the tablet of your heart,
So you will find favor and good repute
In the sight of God and man.
—*Proverbs* 3:3–4

To my own little ones,
who carry my heart around with them
wherever they go.

ONE

The box was plain metal, the color of tarnished silver.

Maddie Lambert watched as Dr. Wrigley slid it carefully onto the bench seat of the jet her father had chartered. He fastened it down with bungee cords. Odd, she thought. The box was so painfully ordinary. She'd imagined it would be more impressive somehow.

Wrigley checked his watch and took a seat on one side of the box, the cabin lights shining on his bald head as he peered at the screen of his phone.

Stomach knotted, she shouldered her bag more firmly and squeezed down the aisle to greet him.

"Dr. Wrigley."

He looked startled. "Ms. Lambert. I had no idea you would be on the flight."

The man hunched on the other end of the bench seat straightened abruptly.

"Paul?" She gasped, momentarily forgetting about Dr. Wrigley and his cargo.

"Maddie."

Two syllables and in them she heard a lifetime of anguish. Maybe the grief was not in his voice, but still ringing in her own ears after a year going on eternity. A wave of emotion shuddered through her so strongly she bit her lip to keep from screaming. They'd agreed to stay out of each other's lives. There was too much pain; the past would forever be an impossible wedge between them. She fought to keep her voice steady. "What are you doing on this plane, Paul?"

Dr. Paul Ford stood, tall and lanky, and shook away the hair that perpetually hung in his eyes. Wrigley eyed them both as if they were a couple of live grenades just rolled down the aisle.

Paul raised his hand slightly, as if he meant to take her cold fingers in his.

She tightened her grip on the bag, nails digging into the nylon strap, and forced herself to stare into his gray eyes.

Paul shoved his hands into the pockets of his jeans, his gaze roving her face as if he had left something there long ago. "I wanted to be here, unofficially, to escort Dr. Wrigley, in case he needed anything."

The pilot stepped into the cabin. The copilot peered in from behind him, a concerned look on his face, and holding a carton with two coffees. "Ms. Lambert? Is there a problem? This gentleman showed proper hospital identification. I was told two Bayview employees, a gentleman from the Heartline Corporation rep and you." He looked around. "Nobody from Heartline yet?"

"No," Dr. Wrigley said. "I'm still not certain why the company needed to send someone to accompany their device anyway. The Berlin Heart is a mechanical marvel. There's no way we would let anything happen to it."

"My father and I expected the hospital director."

The pilot looked again at her. "Shall we delay takeoff?"

Focus, Maddie. Do whatever you need to to get this plane in the air.

"No, there's no problem. I guess the director changed plans."

Paul shrugged. "He canceled."

The pilot excused himself and returned to the cockpit.

Dr. Wrigley looked sharply over his wire-rimmed glasses. "Canceled? Since when?"

Paul seemed not to hear the question. He took a step into the aisle, closer to Maddie. "I didn't think…" He cleared his throat. "I assumed you would have already flown out to be with your father prior to the surgery."

She refused to move back a pace, though his nearness, the musky smell of his cologne made her head spin with too many emotions to name. She felt the bittersweet shadow of lingering tenderness and fought to shut it down. "You think I should be with my father? To say goodbye in case it doesn't work?"

Paul exhaled. "No, to comfort him."

"My sister's there. I wanted to fly with…" She looked at the secured box. "I wanted to be on this flight." She could not stop herself from adding, "After all my father's been through, I thought someone should be there every step along the way."

Paul's face twisted. He looked toward the cockpit, his chin shadowed by dark stubble. The tiny muscles in the corner of his mouth twitched ever so slightly. She looked into his gaze, those gray eyes that used to dance with laughter, and yes, a touch of arrogance, too. They were flat now, as if some internal light had been extinguished.

Dr. Wrigley stood and rested a hand on Paul's shoulder. "Maddie? We've not had a chance to talk in a while. I'm honored to be a part of this. We certainly had to navigate some massive red tape to get hold of a Berlin Heart. Heart-line has only made a few of their artificial hearts this year. Your father picked the best surgeon in the country. I know they had to apply for a compassionate-use permit, since it's not yet cleared by the FDA. If everything goes well, and I'm confident it will, this may be the procedure that ensures

FDA approval. It could save many thousands of lives every year."

It was the time for diplomacy, for a conciliatory tone toward a person so much higher up the ladder she could hardly see him. Instead, she felt the ugly truth spill out. "Dr. Wrigley, I don't care if the Berlin Heart ever gets cleared by the FDA and I don't care about the reputation of the hospital. The only thing on my mind is whether that piece of plastic will save my father's life."

Though it could have been her imagination, she thought she saw the glimmer of a smile on Paul's full lips, though he remained silent.

Dr. Wrigley reddened. "Of course. I can imagine the grief you and your family have endured."

He could imagine? After Wrigley broke up her father's long-ago engagement and knowing her nieces had died in the emergency room he supervised? The anger hummed inside, growing louder with every passing second. "You have grand-children, don't you, Dr. Wrigley?"

He nodded.

"So you're saying you can imagine what it would be like driving them to the park and having a drunk driver plow into your car?"

Paul grimaced, crossing his arms across his chest.

Wrigley's lips tightened. "The hospital and Dr. Ford did the best they could for your nieces, as well as your father."

"Yet, my nieces are dead, while the drunk who hit them is in perfect health." She shot a look at Paul.

The gray of his eyes darkened like a coming storm, but he did not comment.

Her words snapped out. "And you hope to save the reputa-tion of your hospital and deflect my father's financial inves-tigation with this groundbreaking surgery."

Dr. Wrigley's mouth fell open. "Ms. Lambert, your father

has had a personal vendetta against me for years, but I had hoped you'd be more reasonable. Your grief doesn't give you an excuse to attack me or the hospital."

Her voice broke, but she persevered. "My father was investigating Bayview because his company was hired to do so, pending a buyout. That's what he does for a living. It wasn't a personal attack on you. As far as my feelings about the matter, I don't need an excuse to grieve. I see their faces every day in dreams and when I'm awake." Her eyes filled but she willed herself not to cry.

Why had the hospital not had enough staff in the E.R. that fateful morning? It had come to light that Paul was late to work because he'd been on the phone trying to check up on his brother, but there had been no answer. If he'd only made contact, perhaps his drunk sibling might not have plowed into the car Bruce Lambert was driving.

The terrible thought occurred to her again. Paul had four victims brought in then. One of them his brother. The children were too far gone to save, according to official hospital reports, but she didn't believe it. Paul had chosen to help his brother at the expense of the children. Her father believed it deep down in his core. And in spite of the love she and Paul had once shared, the anguish she felt, the darkest part of her believed it, too.

Dr. Wrigley shook his head. "As I said, I understand."

Her fury ebbed, leaving a profound fatigue in its wake. Though she spoke to Wrigley, her eyes were riveted on Paul's. "Respectfully, Dr. Wrigley, you couldn't possibly understand."

The captain's voice crackled over the intercom, requesting the passengers buckle up for takeoff. Maddie walked on trembling legs, glad her seat was facing forward and she wouldn't have to spend the flight looking at Paul. Disbelief fogged her mind.

Paul was on the plane. His nearness was a switchblade pressed to her heart, enough to cut but not to sever.

You've put it behind you. Focus on the now, the miracle you've been given, the heart that will save your father's life.

An Asian man with hair down to his shoulders slid into the seat beside her. She guessed him to be in his fifties, though his eyes seemed much younger. "Hello. Almost missed it."

She jumped. "You must be the man from Heartline."

"Yes. You're Bruce Lambert's daughter? A physical therapist, I heard. I might need one after my sprint through the airport."

She did not want to be talking to him or anyone else, but there was no polite way to ignore the man in the cramped space of the small jet. "My clinic is across town. You can look me up when we get back, Mr....?"

He extended his hand. "Tai Jaden. Pleased to meet you. I'm glad our company could provide the heart that will save your father's life."

She gripped his fingers. "Me, too."

He pointed to the illuminated sign. "Better buckle up. It's time to go."

Maddie closed her eyes and tried to sleep as the flight lifted off through clouded San Francisco skies and headed north, but the shudders of the plane and her own worries prevented it. She could feel Paul's presence like a shadow, and she almost wished she'd decided not to board. Her father hadn't wanted her to accompany the heart. Not necessary, he'd said. Fly ahead and meet it on the other end.

But her father was down to his last days, the Berlin Heart his only option; and the past year, he'd been so stricken that he barely worked or accepted comfort from her. She had little to give anyway. She understood about his torn ventricle and the patched aorta that could not be permanently repaired.

But it was not those things alone that put Bruce Lambert a hairbreadth from death. It was grief and the helplessness of a powerful man who realized he could not buy back a single moment of the past. Doctors were surprised he'd survived this far.

Only one thing kept him alive and able to put his plans into action. It wasn't physical or emotional healing. Not coming to terms with the loss. Something darker and infinitely cold.

He might not achieve peace, but he would have his revenge on Wrigley, on the hospital. She swallowed. On Paul. She'd heard him rant. Not enough doctors on duty. Wrigley unable to be located when he should have been supervising the emergency room. Paul's inability or unwillingness to save the children.

She made herself remember. Paul had managed to save his brother, his blood, at the expense of the kids. She'd heard her father say it time and time again, but there was some tiny part, some deep-down whisper in her heart that wondered.

The desire for revenge was the only thing sustaining her father, and if that was what he needed, she would help him get it.

Paul spoke to Dr. Wrigley. She heard the low huskiness of his voice over the whine of the small airplane's air circulation system. Her guilt was palpable, a live thing that slithered through her gut and into her spine until it whispered in her brain.

Her father's vengeance meant everyone responsible for the children's death would pay.

She shivered.

Jaden shot her a glance. "Cold?"

"Just thinking."

He gave her a curious look as the plane banked and sliced through a storm-washed sky.

She closed her eyes and gave herself to sleep.

* * *

They'd been in the air for two hours going on a lifetime. The plane was a six-seater Cessna, and Paul could see Maddie's chestnut hair just over the top of the seat in front of him. He couldn't decide if he had caught the scent of her, the fragrance she always wore that reminded him of cinnamon, or if it was the cruel taunting of his memory.

Dr. Wrigley's surreptitious glances in his direction didn't help him relax. "What?" Paul said finally, turning to him. "What's on your mind?"

"I'm worried."

"About what?"

Wrigley raised an eyebrow. "Flying with an unstable, grief-blinded woman, for one."

"She's not unstable."

"No? Well blaming the hospital and the both of us for the tragedy isn't rational. She's bought into her father's madness. He's had it against me since grad school."

When you had an affair with his fiancée? Paul imagined his own wrath if someone had tried to steal Maddie from him. The pain in his gut reminded him she was not his anymore. He cleared his throat. "She's just here to make sure nothing goes wrong."

Wrigley's eyes narrowed. "And the man from Heartline. Do you know him?"

Paul looked at the passenger he'd been trying to identify since they took off. "No. Maybe Maddie does." He sighed, thinking about how much he'd lost since they'd broken up. It had been a little more than a year since the accident, two months since he'd last spoken to her, and then it was merely a strained conversation outside a lawyer's office. She seeking a civil suit against the drunk driver who killed her nieces, and he in search of any kind of help for the same man, whom, in spite of everything, Paul loved.

His older brother, Mark, who was in prison.

Paul pushed away the ever-present pain and tried to read his book. This one was set in a submarine. The hero a rugged ex-marine who would accept no failure. Big guy, big guns, lots of good one-liners. If only things were so black and white. You wanted something, you worked hard at it and bingo: dreams came true.

He'd learned early on that, in the field of medicine, dogged determination didn't keep damaged hearts beating. Hard work and a brilliant understanding of the human body wasn't enough.

And sometimes love wasn't, either. It was ironic that he could hardly look at Maddie due to the guilt, yet he couldn't stop thinking about her for a single moment. He leaned his head against the cool glass of the window and tried to refocus on the book.

After the okay from the pilot, he saw Dr. Wrigley check his emails.

"It's from Director Stevens—'Sorry I missed the flight. Thanks for "having a heart" and taking my place. Look forward to your report next week. Keep your eyes on that heart.'" Wrigley grimaced. "Funny guy. I thought I'd had enough of his jokes when he pawned off a meeting on me yesterday and flew the memo into my office on a paper airplane. I had better things to do than sit next to a heart all the way to Washington."

Paul smiled at the thought of Dr. Wrigley chasing a paper airplane. He instinctively glanced at the box between them.

Keep your eyes on that heart.

If anything happened to that biomechanical miracle, it would most likely mean death for Bruce Lambert. There would be no time to procure another device, with all the red tape that had to be plowed through, and the unreliable quantity of human transplants made that option unfeasible at this late hour in Bruce's journey.

Paul pictured the powerful man as he had been that night in the emergency room last year—scared, defiant, even through the pain.

And at the news Paul hadn't been able to save the children?

Incalculably angry.

Paul wished that he could lose himself in anger, too, steep in the rage that would drive away darker feelings. The emotion that filled him to overflowing was guilt, wrapped in a terrible sorrow for the children.

For Bruce Lambert.

For his brother Mark.

And most of all for Maddie and what they had lost. Bruce's rage bled into his daughter, proving to Paul that love and anger weren't compatible. One feeling must crystallize at the top, like the unbreakable sheet of ice atop a frozen lake.

Whatever love Maddie had felt for him before the accident was frozen under the icy weight of her fury and her father's.

He should read, take his mind off the stew of memories, but even the rollicking adventure novel didn't stir his interest.

Paul looked out the window, taking in the rugged Cascade Mountains, snowcapped and sharp against the gray sky. The plane dropped below the cloud cover and more of the Washington terrain came into focus. White-capped peaks, the vivid green of trees against the snow. He wondered why they were flying so low.

It reminded him of winters in Yosemite. So crisp, cold. So beautiful it hurt to look at it.

They'd been planning a honeymoon there, at the old Ahwahnee Hotel. He could imagine it so clearly. Moonlight dancing on snow, the bottomless blue of her eyes, her cheeks flushed with her love of him and that irrepressible joy that always filled her. It was that persistent hope and optimism that enabled Maddie to get broken people on their feet again, to will them through the pain of physical therapy and back on track to living. He'd loved her desperately for that.

His ruminations stopped abruptly as the plane lurched violently.

Dr. Wrigley peered around Paul's shoulder. "What was that?"

There was a crash from the cabin and a thud, as if something had slammed into the door.

The pilot's voice came over the radio, garbled and indistinct.

Dr. Wrigley grabbed his arm. "What did he say?"

Paul struggled out of his seat, instinct screaming at him to get to Maddie, as the floor moved beneath his feet.

"Hold on!" His shout was lost in the cacophony of engine noise as the plane dropped.

His gut knew what was happening, even if his brain could not comprehend.

Their plane was going down.

TWO

Maddie was awakened by a strange jumble of noise and a thunderous concussion that would have thrown her from her seat if not for her seat belt. The cabin shuddered and bucked while it filled with a dense black smoke. It seemed as though the floor was the deck of a ship in high seas as it heaved under her feet.

She looked wildly through the smoke. "What's happening?"

Jaden's face was barely visible through the choking blackness. "I think we might have hit a pinnacle of rock. The pilot's trying to keep it in the air."

The words froze her for a moment. "Trying to keep it in the air?" The thought went through her like a knife. *Save the heart.* With frantic fingers, she fumbled at the buckle of her seat belt.

A strong sucking wind pulled everything toward the opposite side of the cabin, now illuminated by the glow of the flame. Where was Paul? Had he been injured? Some papers and a blue blanket whirled by her face. She saw Jaden free his backpack from under the seat in front of him and cradle it like a baby. He looked resigned.

Maddie was not. She would make it down the aisle and get that box. Finally, the catch on the buckle gave and she ripped the seat belt off. The acrid smoke grew denser, expanding into every inch of space above their heads. She kept her head bowed, trying to inhale the cleaner air below, and struggled to her feet.

"Don't," Jaden yelled over the sound of rushing wind. "Your best chance is to stay seated."

Maddie continued on, forced to her hands and knees to avoid the smoke and the bits of broken glass and plastic shooting through the air. She couldn't see Paul. Whatever they'd crashed into struck the rear of the aircraft. What would she find there? Was it a matter of moments before she was killed? Before they all slammed into the mountains and died?

She swallowed hard, her mouth dry, tongue coated with a bitter metallic taste. Something sharp cut through the knee of her pants. A moment later it seemed as though the crazy movement of the floor had tapered off, the cabin almost leveling out. Using the arm of the chair next to her, she pulled herself to her feet.

Out of the darkness, a figure emerged. She didn't recognize Paul at first. His face was bloodied and soot-stained. He scanned the area until he saw her.

"Maddie." He grabbed her and pushed her back into her seat.

"Let me go. I've got to get the box."

"The plane's in trouble," he said. "You need to sit."

She fought against his hands. "Let me go, Paul."

He took her by the shoulders and pressed her harder into the chair.

She struggled in his grasp.

"Stop it, Maddie," he shouted.

In the four years they'd been together she'd never heard him raise his voice. The sound shocked her so much she stopped.

The cabin floor sloped downward suddenly and he almost fell on her lap, landing instead on his knees in the aisle.

He leaned close. "Listen to me. The pilot has lost control for some reason. He must have managed to level us out. He's probably trying to land, but we're headed into the mountains. Do you understand me? If you are going to live through the impact, your best hope is to be buckled up."

She stared at him. "I've got to save the Berlin Heart."

His eyes were the same pearl-gray as the soot that clung to his forehead. "It's safer where it is, instead of flying all over the cabin." He turned to Jaden. "Are you injured?"

Jaden shook his head, face expressionless.

A whine rose above the other noises. With a sharp crack, the window fractured and pulled loose. Paul shielded her body with his.

With her cheek pressed to his chest she could feel the racing of his heart, hear his sharp intake of breath as the glass cut into him from behind. He pulled away.

She searched his face. "Are you hurt?"

He ignored the question, bending over to buckle the seat belt around her waist. His voice was quieter now. "Please stay here, Maddie. I'm going to see if I can help Dr. Wrigley."

Through the hole where the window had been, freezing air barreled in. Alternate streaks of white and green flashed by, pine trees against a blanket of snow. Close. Too close.

She did not fight any more. "I'll do it, but only if you stay here, too."

He gave her a quizzical look. Then he rubbed a hand across his face, smearing the soot into oozy spirals. Without a word, he moved to take the seat behind her, but before he did he pulled a blanket loose and tucked it around her, giving her a corner to hold. "Protect your face from any flying glass."

The blanket smelled of singed plastic, but she huddled behind it anyway, thinking she must be in the grip of a powerful nightmare. It could not be true that she was sitting in a crashing plane, and the device that would save her father's life was going down with it. Not now, not when she had a chance to fix things.

She eased the blanket aside and peeked behind her at Paul, eyes closed, lips moving.

He was praying to a God she used to know, a God that let little children die in pain and adults live in agony.

The pain swirled inside her with vicious intensity. She wished in that moment she still had someone to pray to, to help her with the fear that choked the breath out of her.

When Paul was done, he opened his eyes and looked out the window. "It won't be long now," he said.

He didn't look scared, only perplexed, as if he wondered how he came to be aboard a crashing plane. Absently, he patted the pocket of his coat.

"What are you looking for?"

He started, then grinned. "Candy."

She knew he'd given up smoking at age nineteen and developed a ferocious candy habit, encouraged by long nights eating out of vending machines at the hospital. The gesture brought tears to her eyes for a reason she couldn't understand. "Paul, are we going to die?"

His expression was one of myriad emotions, probably the same ones he showed to families when there was no hope to give, no comfort left to offer. He pushed his hand through the gap between the chairs and squeezed her hand. "We'll make it."

She was grateful for the lie.

Paul watched as the ground loomed closer with every passing moment. The smoke that filled the cabin made it impossible to see Dr. Wrigley or Maddie's seatmate as they careened on. He couldn't hear anything over the deafening roar of the dying aircraft.

They were low enough now that the trees slapped and crunched under the belly of the plane. He suspected the pilot was either unconscious or disabled. Paul wished for a crazy moment that he had the arsenal of skills of the ex-marine in the novel. He could take over the controls and find a flat spot to land. The galling reality was, he was powerless to do anything. He had no idea how to fly a plane, and the cockpit doors were reinforced against any kind of breach, and if two experienced pilots couldn't land it, neither could he.

Another window ripped free and hurtled through the cabin behind them. With a wild swing of his arm, he batted it away from Maddie. She was huddled under the blanket. He was glad. Better for her not to see the mountain rushing up at them.

Ironically, he remembered the last airplane-crash victim he'd treated. It was a nine-month-old baby who survived the horror with only a slight scratch on her cheek. Rescuers named her Sunny, since she greeted them in the midst of the smoke and fire with a tiny-toothed smile.

Her parents hadn't been so lucky.

He considered trying to free his cell and call someone to alert them of their location, but he didn't think he could hold the phone steady against the vicious tremors of the plane.

The wing struck a projection of rock and spun around, cartwheeling them into dizzying circles. The whirling dislodged cushions and broken equipment, hurling them around the cabin. Metal gave way and a fissure ripped through the roof, raining a mixture of hot steel and freezing snow down on them.

Maddie screamed.

He shouted to her, but the din covered his words. The only

thing he could do was grip her shoulder around the side of the seat and ask God to spare her.

She'd been through enough.

Her father had, too, and Paul knew Berlin Heart or no Berlin Heart, Bruce Lambert wouldn't survive the death of his daughter.

The plane flipped and rolled. Paul heard the sound of shearing metal and he hoped the seats were not ripping loose from the floor. Another crack appeared in the ceiling. The aircraft was beginning to break apart.

"Paul!" Maddie screamed. "We're—"

Her words were snatched away in the wind.

The whine of the engines stopped abruptly. His stomach fell as the plane began a steep dive to the ground. He held on to her until the turbulence tore them apart. The grinding of metal sounded from under their feet and Paul watched in horror as Maddie's seat began to shudder from its moorings.

He tried to unbuckle himself to grab at her chair, to somehow keep her anchored to him through what was to come, but his own seat pulled loose and he was pitched backward into the smoke-filled rear of the craft.

There was a final, bone-jarring impact, a bombardment of burning shards and jagged metal, and the plane slammed into the ground.

Flickers of color appeared in front of Maddie's eyes as she blinked back to consciousness. Black smoke and white snow. Her brain fought to make sense of it. Neatly strapped into her seat, yet feeling the sting of icy flakes on her arms? The terrible noise was gone, replaced by an eerie silence broken only by the rush of wind and a crackling she could not identify. The smoke cleared enough for her to assess the situation.

She was in her seat, yes, but the seat was loose, tumbled to the side of a section of aircraft that had broken away from the main body of the plane. From her semiupright position, she looked out onto the snow, dotted with dark pockets of still-smoking debris. Frigid air seared her lungs as she fumbled for the seat-belt release. She had somehow survived the crash.

Had Paul? She could still feel his hands clutching her, trying to keep her from whirling away.

There was no sign of him in the smoke-filled gloom.

She did not know whether to feel grateful or afraid.

She gritted her teeth as the buckle came loose. Half stupefied with fear, she forced herself to look at her body. There was no obvious bleeding, no pain to indicate she'd suffered a traumatic blow. Slowly, she wiggled both feet and gingerly moved her legs. Aside from myriad cuts and abrasions, her body appeared to be working fine. Pressing a hand to her temple, she felt the warm trickle of blood and a dull ache in her wrist. Jaw clenched, she struggled to her feet, head ducked low under the twisted fragment of the plane. She shuffled to the opening, still taking inventory of her injuries. As she approached the lip of the shredded cabin, her stomach tightened.

What would she find tangled in the twisted metal?

Dr. Wrigley?

Tai Jaden?

She swallowed hard. Paul?

And what had become of the Berlin Heart?

Her instincts screamed at her not to cross that smoking threshold.

Stay in shelter. Stay away from the gruesome sights that might be waiting.

Still, she found herself drawn to the opening.

The cold air hit her like a fist, her eyes tearing, vision blurred.

She blinked them away. The piece of the wreckage she

stood in was cratered on a snowy hill, wedged against a stand of pines that must have stopped the chunk of wreckage from sliding any farther. Plumes of steam rose from the snow where grotesquely twisted shards of metal protruded like the skeleton of some long-dead thing. She couldn't see any more pieces of intact plane from her position. The impact must have thrown her some distance.

Wishing she had managed to hold on to her purse, she fumbled in her pocket and retrieved the cell phone.

Please work. Please work.

No signal available, the screen read. She would not be summoning help, or calling Paul. Maybe it was a blessing, anyway. What would it be like to hear Paul's phone ring endlessly, imagining all the reasons why he was not able to answer? What would it be like to know she would never hear his voice again? Those ridiculous ideas that made her groan. The Donald Duck impressions he did for his young patients.

Her breath froze.

Perhaps the rest of the plane had disintegrated and she was the only one, the only survivor.

The thought paralyzed her until she balled the fear up in her mind and transformed it into rage, penetrating and intense as the cold all around her.

No. It wouldn't be death for all these innocent people.

"That's not the way it's going to end." She hadn't realized she'd shouted aloud until the words echoed back to her. It was time to go find the others and help them.

She put out a hand to brace herself for the climb down, but yanked her fingers away when the metal burned her skin. Grabbing a couple of blackened cushions, she held one in front of her and sat on the other, skidding down the side of the plane.

Even with the fabric insulation, she could feel the heat

seep into her pants. When her feet crunched into knee-deep snow, she floundered for a moment before she climbed up on a wide section of metal lying on the ground, grateful it wasn't smoking hot. The realization hit her. It was a section of wing, broken loose.

Scooting out as far as the metal surface would allow, she peered through the smoke. Just south of her was a deep furrow of snow, gouged wide, until it disappeared over the rise ahead. She walked to the end of the wingtip and stepped off gingerly, sinking again into the whiteness. Ignoring the chill, she made her way laboriously toward the edge of the slope where she would be able to get a view of what lay below.

Stomach knotted, muscles complaining with every step, she moved on, wishing she had more than a wool blazer for warmth. The edge neared, and in spite of her earlier bravado, fear nibbled at the corners of her mind. What would she find? How could he have survived?

She realized she was thinking not of Wrigley or Jaden, but of Paul. Only of Paul.

The anger she nursed was alive as ever, bitter as gall, yet fear rose up right alongside it.

She wanted to shout, to tear through the oppressive stillness and hear the comfort of a reply. Far worse would be an answering silence. Shuddering, skin prickled with goose bumps, she forced her feet to the top of the rise.

Looking down with eyes streaming from the acrid smoke that filled the air, she saw the rest of the plane, upside down, half-buried in snow. There was no sign of movement from inside.

She continued on. Downslope, the snow was harder, fused into sheets of icy crust.

Her mind wandered back to her nieces, Ginny and Beth, on their annual trip to Bear Valley. The shrill cries of Ginny as she raced along on a toboggan with her sister close behind,

Maddie's sister, Katie, watching, eyes dancing, Maddie waiting at the bottom, where Katie's husband, Roger, should have been if he hadn't had an affair that ended their marriage. Katie had once told Maddie she wondered if his affair wasn't a reaction to his Huntington's disease diagnosis.

Maddie refused to listen. Katie had to deal not only with Roger's life-altering diagnosis, but the terror of wondering if the girls had inherited the disease. And she'd never considered having an affair. Roger had been weak and selfish. When he left, Maddie tried to fill in for him as much as she could. They'd made their own odd little family, bound together by love and loss, and always overseeing everything was Bruce Lambert, father, grandfather and steadfast rock.

The moisture on her face hardened into icy trails, and she scraped them away as she tried to inject some logical thinking into her half-frozen mind.

She had no idea how much time had passed since the accident, or if their sudden disappearance off the radar had been noticed by airport officials. Was there a rescue crew on the way? Had her father and sister been alerted?

She hoped her family hadn't been told. The worry could prove too much for her father's damaged heart.

Gritting her teeth, she pressed on. The Berlin Heart would be in this section, and if she could save it, the rescuers would be able to get it to her dad. Her own heart tumbled in her chest as she drew closer to the wreck. Her feet were so cold in her leather slip-ons, she felt as if she were walking on two frozen stumps.

How long before frostbite would begin to kill her extremities, she wondered? Fifty feet away, and she could see the details now. Windows blown out, sharp twists of metal, blackened bits of plastic littered like flakes of pepper on salt-white snow.

A plume of flame erupted from behind one of the windows.

Maddie screamed, the sound echoing through the snowy hollow. She waited to see if the flames would escalate into a roaring inferno, but they died away again.

She had to get in there and find Paul and Dr. Wrigley and the heart, before it was too late.

In spite of her determination, she stopped again.

The images of other deaths came back to her in all their brutality. When the girls died, it kindled an impenetrable fear inside Maddie that froze her in her tracks. She'd once armored herself against that fear with faith, but it had been ripped away in the moments after the car crash, leaving her soul tattered and exposed.

The fear had rooted deep then.

And threatened to overwhelm her now.

She could not move.

Another plume of flame erupted from a different location, bringing with it black smoke that swirled through the open side of the plane.

Through the haze, a man staggered out.

Maddie's heart thundered and she reached a hand toward him. "Here."

She could not tell if he reacted to her voice, or if he even heard her as he fell facedown in the snow.

THREE

Breaking free of her numbing paralysis, she ran, falling and floundering, through the snow. He was so covered with black that she could not tell his identity at first, until she saw the twisted glasses lying next to him.

Dr. Wrigley.

Not allowing herself to acknowledge the keen surge of disappointment, she rolled him over as gently as she could, to prevent him from suffocating in the snow. His eyelids fluttered as he came to.

"What...?"

"Our plane crashed. Are you badly injured?"

He blinked and struggled to sit up. She considered pushing him back to keep him from further injury, but exposure to the icy ground would kill him as certainly as any internal damage. She helped him sit up.

He clutched a hand to his front. "I think my clavicle is broken."

She didn't dare peel away any layers of clothing to assess. "We've got to get to shelter somehow. Have—did you see what happened to Paul or the other passenger?"

Wrigley gently bent his glasses back into position and put them on. "No. I didn't see anyone inside. But the smoke was so thick."

He scrambled to his knees, sliding against the slick surface as she helped him to his feet. They moved to the shelter of a copse of fir trees.

Maddie made sure he was not going into shock before she turned away. "I'm going back. Stay here."

Wrigley stiffened as if he wasn't used to taking orders. "Going back in there? The plane is on fire. We need to stay away before it blows."

The flames were visible now, dancing through the shattered windows.

"Not until I know about the survivors and I get my father's heart."

He didn't raise a hand to stop her, and she moved quickly toward the burning wreck.

The smoke was thicker now, as she approached the threshold. An overnight bag flew out the opening, almost knocking her over.

Another followed.

"Hey," she managed.

Tai Jaden appeared in the opening. He gaped at her.

"You made it." He shook his head. "I can't believe anybody did. The plane is shredded."

"Dr. Wrigley is alive." She watched him pull out blankets and toss them onto the snow. "What are you doing?"

"We've gotta get any warm clothes and supplies out of here before it goes up in flames."

"I need the Berlin Heart."

His eyes glittered in the dim light. "I'll get it."

"Where's Paul? Have you seen him?"

"The tall guy who was with Dr. Wrigley?"

"Yes."

Jaden looked around, prowling between the piles of loosened seats. "He's not in here. Could have been thrown out when the plane cracked apart. Some of the seats are just plain gone, from what I can see. The rear is hard to get to, but maybe I can access it from the tail end. I'll look for the box, and then we'll find him." Jaden disappeared back inside.

Maddie's mind raced. Then Paul might be lying somewhere in the snow, covered by wreckage. Had she passed right by him and not known? She felt a surge of anger. He shouldn't have even been on the plane. He had no reason to be a part of her life anymore.

Still, she strained her eyes through the smoke and the curtain of snow that had begun to fall. He'd been right behind her, or so she'd thought, but it was clear he was not in the wreckage now. The side they'd sat on was crushed against the ground. Had he been thrown clear? The only way to get a good look was to move around to the other side of the plane. Floundering in deep pockets of snow, she traced the perimeter of the tail end, though the rudder appeared to have been sheared off. The smoke nearly blinded her, and she kept her head down to avoid breathing the toxic fumes.

The crackle of flames grew louder, along with the sound of Jaden throwing bags off the plane. He would find the Berlin Heart; and if he didn't she would get it herself, after she found Paul. She tried to move faster, but the snow seemed to pull her down. The glint of glass shone in the sunlight, and Maddie arrived at the cockpit.

The pilots.

She realized with a start that she hadn't given a thought to their fate.

Teeth clenched, she peered in.

The glass was veined with cracks, the far door twisted off, allowing cold air to find its way in. There was no one inside.

More missing people, she thought.

A sound caught her attention, a half shout that died away abruptly. It came from the bottom of a small, snow-covered hill. She didn't wait to hear more. Trying to run, Maddie slipped and skidded until she crested the hill and looked down to find two men, one prone, one on his knees.

Terror filled her, thick and weighty, as she tumbled toward them.

Paul looked up from his examination of the pilot, and felt a relief so profound he thought it might drown him. For a moment, he couldn't get the words out. "Maddie. I looked everywhere to find you. I thought…"

Maddie closed her eyes for a moment and wrapped her arms around herself. He thought he saw tears glistening on her face, but decided it must be the dazzle of sun and snow.

She was alive. *Alive.* He wanted to grab hold and crush her in his arms, but instead he continued to monitor the pilot's breathing, his hands suddenly shaking. "Are you hurt?"

"I'm okay. Jaden is, too. Wrigley's hurt, but alive. What about you?"

He felt buoyed by the thought that the four of them had miraculously survived. "Couple of cracked ribs, I think. I was looking for you and I found the pilot wandering. The copilot is dead. I saw him under a chunk of wreckage, but I couldn't move it."

The pilot's face was ashen, and his lips moved.

Paul bent low. "I'm here, buddy. Right here. You're going to be okay."

His lips moved several times before the words came out. "I think…coffee was drugged."

Paul looked at Maddie, whose face showed shock and disbelief.

"Did he say…?" Maddie started.

Paul gently lifted the man's eyelids. "His pupils are dilated. It could be from a narcotic or a concussion." Drugged? He didn't have time to think more about it as the pilot's breathing died and his heartbeat fluttered to a halt. The man was in cardiac arrest. Paul immediately began chest compressions.

Maddie knelt next to him and gave the man two breaths.

They kept up a full cycle of CPR before Maddie felt for a pulse. "Nothing."

Paul continued, feeling guilty that he was so happy to see Maddie while a man lay in cardiac arrest before him. He couldn't stop himself from thinking it. *Thank You, God, for sparing her life.* Above all things, he did not want to find her dead or dying in the wreckage. And now she knelt next to him, cheeks pink, breath making puffs in the cold air.

Maddie was alive. When he brought the pilot back, there would be only one fatality from the horrific crash. They'd wait for rescue. They would all survive.

He was so lost in the feeling, he didn't hear her at first.

"Still no heartbeat."

Paul blinked. "What?"

Maddie gestured to the pilot. "No heartbeat, Paul. Nothing."

Jaden joined them. "Took me a while to find you. What can I do?"

Paul waited to answer until Maddie was giving the rescue breaths. "Do you have any medical training?"

"No, I'm just a Heartline rep."

Paul nodded. "Can you find a tarp or piece of plastic? Anything we can use to get him off this snow?"

Jaden hesitated a moment before he disappeared over the rise.

Maddie touched Paul's arm. "Paul, I don't think you're going to save him."

Paul shook his head. "Hasn't been down that long. I can get him started." Though his arms were aching with fatigue, and each movement aggravated his ribs and made the wounds on his back sting, Paul kept on. "One-one-thousand, two-one-thousand," he counted with each thrust of his hands on the man's chest.

Maddie gave the next set of breaths, though the urgency seemed to have gone out of her. Didn't matter. She wasn't a doctor. She didn't know the wildly persistent quality of human life. He'd seen people in comas suddenly wake up when doctors said there was no hope. He'd known small children to survive inhuman conditions with smiles on their faces.

A part of him filled in the rest.

And you've also seen plenty of people you couldn't save with any amount of effort.

Not this time.

The pilot's name was N. Fisher. The man thought he had been drugged, if he'd heard right, yet somehow the guy had managed to get them down alive. Paul recalled the scuffle he'd heard in the cabin and wondered about the copilot's part in the crash. He steeled his arms and did the compressions more aggressively.

The next time he looked up, Jaden was there, and Dr. Wrigley.

Dr. Wrigley looked at him from behind glasses that sat slightly cockeyed on his face. "Dr. Ford, your patient is gone. You need to call it."

"No," Paul said, feeling his stomach clench. "I can get him back."

"Four-one-thousand, five-one-thousand." His shoulder muscles screamed at him, his injured ribs stabbing at him with every movement. The end of the cycle came and he looked to Maddie. Her face was damp with tears.

"It's over, Paul."

Anger surged inside him. "I'm a doctor. I know when it's time to quit. I say I can save him."

He pushed past her and administered the two rescue breaths himself. When he returned for compressions, Dr.

Wrigley took a step forward and gripped his upper arm with surprising strength.

"Dr. Ford, the pilot is dead. There is no hope of resuscitation, in spite of your efforts." He looked at his watch. "The time of death is ten-fifteen a.m."

Paul looked at them and read it in their faces. He knew they were right. He was not going to make a save this time. Despair rose inside, along with a deep fatigue. He slowly got to his feet and Jaden stepped forward with a blanket he'd retrieved, draping the body against the falling snow.

Paul stood, hands on hips. "His name was Fisher. I saw it on his ID tag. He saved us."

Maddie looked at the ground when she spoke. "You did your best."

The irony cut deep. *I did my best for your nieces, too. Had* he?

The question that had tormented him every day since the crash surfaced again. Had he done everything medically possible for the children? Was there something he'd overlooked because he'd been distracted by another accident victim, his brother? He'd replayed the events second by painful second in his mind, without achieving any clarity. The bald facts were that today the children were gone, Bruce Lambert was hanging on by his fingernails and Paul's brother, Mark, was in perfect health.

A cold wind struck at them and he saw Maddie shiver. "We've got to get some shelter and wait for a rescue team."

Jaden looked around. "The cabin is unstable, and there's a fire burning in the electrical system. I salvaged what I could, but we can't take cover there."

Wrigley took a few steps toward the top of the hill. "There must be something nearby. A cave, a cabin—something."

Paul considered. "I think the best bet is to move to the bottom of that rock wall. If we can find some debris to stand on, maybe some wood to make a fire, we can at least be out of the wind."

"I'll get the gear that survived and see if there's anything else." Jaden zipped his jacket up to his chin, against the biting wind.

Maddie nodded. "I'll help. I've got to make sure the Berlin Heart is safe."

An odd look crossed Jaden's face, but Paul could not read it before the man turned and headed quickly up the hill. Maddie followed, struggling to keep up.

The Berlin Heart. He'd forgotten all about it. The rescue team might still be able to fly it to Bruce's hospital. He looked ahead at the smoke rising from the downed plane. Had it been damaged? He didn't allow his mind to continue the thought. *One catastrophe at a time, Ford.*

Before he followed Maddie up hill, he bent to one knee again and said a prayer for N. Fisher.

Dr. Wrigley stayed with the pile of singed carry-on bags while Jaden and Paul approached the plane, Maddie following. Her thoughts were fuzzy as she moved to climb on the wreckage. She'd just seen a man die, and though all she knew about him was his last name, she couldn't ignore a feeling of loss. She wondered if Paul felt it every time he lost a patient. Maybe he felt it more keenly when he'd sacrificed one patient for the next, as he'd done with her nieces. Her father's words rang in her memory.

He let them die, Maddie. He let the girls die.

Thinking of her dad drove all thoughts about Paul away.

Her face was stiff with cold, and she reached carefully to hold on where the metal was not sheared off razor-sharp. Smoke continued to blossom out of the shattered windows and the crackle of flames was louder now.

She was about to haul herself up when Paul stopped her.

He put a hand on her shoulder. "Don't go in there."

His face was calm again, unmarked with the same frustration and anger she'd seen a moment before.

"I'm going, Paul."

"Not a good idea. The smoke is toxic, you know that."

She yanked out of his grasp. "I'm not going to let my father die."

Jaden appeared in the opening. "Fire's getting closer to the fuel tanks. We've gotta clear out."

Maddie called over the crackling. "Did you get the heart?"

She didn't hear his reply as a whooshing noise filled the air.

Paul grabbed her wrist and pulled her away from the wreck.

She fought him, twisting and jerking. "Let go of me."

She thought he'd listened for a moment, until she found herself draped like an ungainly package over his shoulder. Squirming did nothing to loosen his grip.

"Fight all you want, Maddie. I'm not going to let you die."

She watched his feet crunch through the snow. "I hate you, Paul," she stormed, angry tears bursting from her eyes.

He sighed. "I know, Mads."

The grief in his voice startled her. Before she could say anything else, he'd lowered her to the ground next to Dr. Wrigley and started to jog back to the plane.

Maddie wanted nothing more than to march over to the plane and let him have it. She settled for kicking a mound of snow into icy smithereens.

Wrigley didn't comment as he watched her, but she could see the corner of his mouth crimp and the thought that he was amused infuriated her all the more. He handed her a bag.

"I believe this is yours. Do you have warmer clothes in there?"

She grabbed it from his hands. "Yes. But I can wait until the plane is unloaded."

"At least put boots on if you've got them." He pointed to her feet. "Frostbite sets in quickly, and we've been in the snow for a while now. I'm glad I found mine." He looked as though he was going to cry for a moment.

The emotion unsettled her. To give herself something to do, she fished through the blackened carry-on until she found socks and her snow boots. The irony stung. She'd planned a long walk with her sister after their father's surgery was completed. A time when they could share their grief, but with the added promise of a more hopeful future.

She yanked on the boots. She'd have it all, just like she'd planned.

Though her feet were numb with the cold, it was a relief to have the thick soles between her toes and the rapidly piling snow. Dr. Wrigley stiffened, his eyes riveted to the twisted remnants of the plane.

"What?" she said, trying to follow his gaze.

She saw Jaden and Paul dive out of the opening into the pile of luggage they'd retrieved.

After a few seconds' delay, the structure erupted into an orange fireball. It was an explosion that deafened Maddie, and she threw her hands around her head as the air became unbearably hot.

When the noise and heat subsided enough for her to raise her face, she was relieved to see Jaden and Paul heaving themselves to their feet. Each man grabbed an armful of rescued belongings and made their way back to join the others.

Maddie couldn't wait for them to cross the hundred yards. She ran and met them, nerves tingling, stomach constricted. "Did you get it out? Did you get the Berlin Heart?"

Jaden wiped a sooty hand across his face but didn't answer.

"Tell me," Maddie all but shrieked. "You found it, didn't you?"

Paul made a small movement toward her. "Yes, we found it."

Her breath whooshed out of her, the relief so profound she could feel it in every pore of her body. "Thank goodness. Where is it?"

"Maddie…" Paul said.

They weren't carrying the box. It must be in the pile they hurled just before the plane exploded. She darted toward the wreck, shielding her face from the heat. "I've got to move it away from the fire."

Paul put the gear down and followed her. "Maddie, it's not there."

She continued on, eyes searching, straining for a glimpse of the metal box. "Leave me alone, Paul."

He spoke louder. "We couldn't get it."

The intensity finally penetrated. "What do you mean? You said you found it."

Paul looked at her and she could see the flames mirrored in his eyes.

"The metal shell of the tail section collapsed in on itself while we searched. It's welded shut from the heat. We couldn't get to it. We couldn't save your father's heart."

FOUR

Paul ignored the snow that fell in a steady curtain around him. He had eyes only for Maddie and the anguish that played over her face. She took a step backward and he thought she would tumble, so he reached out a hand for her.

She stiffened. "Please," she whispered. "Leave me alone." She turned and walked to the shelter of a thick pine tree. Her shoulders slumped, head down, defeat written in the lines of her body.

Paul started after her, but Jaden stopped him. "Let her have a minute, Dr. Ford."

"She's hurting."

Jaden shrugged. "If we don't come up with a plan here pretty quick, it isn't going to matter."

Paul stared at Jaden and then at Dr. Wrigley, who cradled his shoulder and grimaced. The snow fell harder, piling into puffs around them. The sky darkened to a dull slate, though Paul's cracked watch showed the time to be just after noon. He shot one more glance at Maddie. She hadn't moved. He fought the urge to go to her. It was time to start thinking triage, prioritize what they would need to do to keep all four of them alive. "Okay. Let's talk this out."

Jaden nodded. "Search-and-rescue is probably mobilizing, but it may take a while for them to find us, and there's a storm coming, so they won't risk losing aircraft. I'm guessing we're on our own at least until morning."

Paul raised an eyebrow. "You former military or something?"

A glimmer of a smile played on Jaden's lips. "You wouldn't believe the great training Heartline provides its employees."

Paul folded his arms. "Uh-huh." He turned his focus to the surroundings. The temperature was dropping steadily, and exposure would kill them first. He scanned the terrain. Steep snow-covered slopes rose on either side, studded with enormous trees. The main body of the plane was now completely engulfed in flame, belching out toxic smoke into the thin air.

Paul reviewed the survival training he'd taken in his backpacking phase. "Shelter first. We've got to find something to get us out of the storm." As he spoke, he removed his belt and buckled it into a circle. He hung it over Wrigley's neck and helped him gingerly rest his injured arm in the makeshift sling. Wrigley nodded his thanks, his face pained.

Jaden grunted. "Right. Dr. Wrigley, keep moving around, see if you can get a signal on your phone. It's doubtful, but worth trying." He pointed to a ridge of rock that thrust upward through the snow. "Let's check there for any kind of covered area."

"I'm on it." Paul made sure Maddie was still safe under the tree before he plowed through the snow toward the shadowed rocks. Sinking to his knees every few steps, Paul floundered along until he reached the base of the rock which had long ago tumbled loose from the towering mountain peak. He picked his way from one rock—up and over—onto the next, in search of some indentation, any kind of rocky depression that might screen them from the elements.

He slipped on an iced-over patch and loosened a shower of rubble that rained down onto the snow.

Careful, Ford. Let's not get taken out by a bunch of rocks, especially when you just survived a plane crash. That part still seemed surreal. Had the pilot really said he'd been drugged? The sinister notion added to the tension in his gut, but Paul put them away for later. He had to find shelter for Maddie.

What scared him more than the crash, more than the notion that someone wanted them to die, was the defeat on her face. The Berlin Heart was lost, and it seemed her father was, too. Could she live through it? After the death of her nieces?

He climbed over a sharp projection of rock. Part of Maddie had died the day the children did, and truth be told, part of him had, as well. He'd lost some of his confidence—some might say arrogance—when he could not save those girls. He shook the thought away, along with a clump of snow that attached itself to his neck.

Help me find a way, Lord.

The snow coated his hair now, freezing his coat stiff against his complaining muscles and aching ribs. Dropping down behind a pile of black rock, he found nothing, just a smooth blanket of white. It reminded him of backpacking trips with his big brother, Mark, especially the time Paul broke his foot, diving into a tree trunk hidden in the water, and Mark carried him five miles back to their uncle's place, cracking jokes all the while. Mark was always quick with a one-liner, even now that they only saw each other across a scarred table in the prison visiting area, but Paul saw the pain in his brother's eyes.

The question that haunted him daily surfaced in his mind. Would things have been different if Mark hadn't been exposed to his uncle's cavalier attitude toward alcohol at a vulnerable time in his life?

You're a physician, Paul. You know that alcoholism is a disease that can affect people anywhere, anytime, regardless of the situation. Still, if his father hadn't left them…if Uncle Lyman hadn't turned a blind eye to Mark's drinking…

If, if, if.

None of it would change a thing. The indisputable fact was, Mark was driving the car that hit Bruce Lambert and the kids, and he had been drinking. For all his protestations that another car had been involved, the police could not find evidence to support Mark's claim. Their case was cut-and-dried. Mark drove drunk. He plowed into the Lamberts' car. He was guilty of manslaughter.

And the other indisputable fact was that Paul had loaned the car that morning to his brother, thinking that this time, finally, his brother really had sobered up.

A piece of rock came loose in Paul's hand and he threw it savagely as far as he could. He didn't even hear it land. Biting back the frustration, he shook the snow from his hair and started to climb back up to search in another direction, when he noticed a hole cut into the rock, about four feet across. Icicles hung from the rim, like jagged teeth.

With nothing to lose, Paul kicked at the icicles to break them off and stuck his head into the opening. Blinking to be sure he was not the victim of a hallucination, he peered into the gloom again before he said a silent thank-you and headed back to the others. Finally, one small thing had gone right.

Maddie saw the snow deepening around her, but she could not feel it. Her body was numb from the inside out, with a bitter cold that had nothing to do with the elements. In the distance, the plane crackled and hissed, as if it hid some creature living out its last breath.

Last breath.

Last hope.

She was trapped in a surreal nightmare. The marvelous machine that would save her father was lying crushed underneath a half ton of twisted wreckage. She wanted to be angry at the pilot for letting them crash, at Jaden and Paul for not saving the heart; but deep down she knew they were not to blame.

Each breath caused a pain that cut her open inside.

The harsh truth was, she could have gone to get the heart, but her need to find Paul drove her to him instead. If she had put her father first, as he had done for her all her life, she would have gotten the device off the plane before it exploded.

Could it be true? Had she really sacrificed her father's life for Paul? The man who already held responsibility for letting her nieces die? *Paul, Paul, Paul.* He was the center of all her pain, and now there was no chance that she would ever be able to rebuild the tattered remnants of her life.

She felt herself sliding to the ground. Snow crunched under her as she collapsed on hands and knees, her palms punching down through the iced crust. There should have been tears, rivers of them, flowing hot down her face, but there were none. There was no way to release the terrible agony she felt, not a single tear left to ease the pain.

A hand took her arm and pulled her up. Tai Jaden stood over her, brows drawn together, saying something. But she couldn't understand him through the wind and the emotion howling through her body.

She didn't want to go with him, but he moved her anyway, until she found herself sitting on a pile of luggage.

"Watch her," Jaden told Dr. Wrigley. "I'm going to see what Paul found."

Dr. Wrigley eyed her uneasily as his fingers moved over the keys on his phone. "No signal still. It's like we're at the bottom of a well."

She didn't answer. Instead, she looked at the fire, still burning, and wondered how long her father had left to live.

"We'll make it. The rescue crew will find us soon," Wrigley said.

She wondered if he was saying the words to comfort her or himself. A nod was all she could manage.

When Jaden returned, Paul came with him, cheeks reddened and jacket dusted with snow. He hastened to Maddie.

"There's a cave back behind those rocks. We'll have some shelter there until help arrives."

She looked at him, at the face that had brought her so much hope and joy in the past. A desperate thought took root in her mind. She grasped his hand. "Paul."

He started and covered her fingers with his, chafing as if to rub some life back into them. "What is it, Mads?"

"Is there a chance, any chance, that we could get another Berlin Heart for my father?"

Paul opened his mouth, then closed it. He squeezed her hand. "There's always a chance."

But she saw the truth in his eyes. It had taken months of effort on the part of the hospital and her father's government contacts to obtain one Berlin Heart. People in Europe and the States were vying for the precious few that were produced. Months that Bruce Lambert did not have anymore. Her father's best hope was entombed in a burning aircraft, a medical marvel with all the hope smashed out of it, just like herself.

She looked away, biting down on her lip until she tasted blood.

He tried to put an arm around her, but she shook him off. She would not take comfort from him, or anyone, ever again.

Dr. Wrigley grabbed a suitcase with his good arm. Jaden and Paul did the same. In a daze, Maddie picked up the bag

she'd been sitting on and followed them. Someone helped
her over a steep rock and another took the luggage while she
ducked under the rounded archway and stepped into the large
cave. The ground was clear of snow, covered with rocks from
pea-size to boulders. The ceiling rose ten feet above them,
glazed and shimmering, as if it had been carved out of ice.
It was deep, so deep the far walls were bathed in darkness.

Paul ushered her to the far side, away from the entrance,
and urged her to sit on a blanket he'd placed on a piece of
luggage. The others did the same, moving together until they
were seated in a strange circle, as if they were enjoying a
camping trip instead of having just fallen out of the sky.

Jaden looked around. "Ice cave?"

Paul spoke, his breath making steamy trails in the cold air.
"Caused by steam, I'd guess. This mountain is volcanic. The
rising heat melted these tunnels in the glacial ice. I'd guess
there's a network of them."

Wrigley sighed. "Too bad it isn't any warmer than outside."

"At least we're out of the snow." Paul rummaged in his
pack. "Is everyone okay? I found a small first-aid kit, and I
can take care of any minor injuries."

Jaden waved him off. Dr. Wrigley pointed to his shoulder.
"I believe my clavicle is broken."

Paul nodded. "I'll make a better sling to immobilize it."
He turned to Maddie, his voice soft. "Is there anything I can
do for you?"

She shook her head, unable to trust her voice. He continued
to look at her, his gaze deep and searching, but she lowered
her eyes to stare at the ground.

Paul unrolled a length of linen from the kit and began to
fasten it around Dr. Wrigley's neck. "I need to tell you all
something Maddie and I heard from the pilot before he died.
It's not good news."

Wrigley grimaced. "How could it be worse at this point?"

"The pilot said his coffee had been drugged."

Jaden stiffened. "Drugged? Is that what caused the crash?"

Paul sighed wearily. "I would guess so. Seems to fit the facts. His depth perception was probably off. He clipped the mountain, fought off the effects of the drug long enough to straighten us out, but not enough to keep from crashing."

"The copilot, too?" Jaden asked.

Paul shook his head. "I don't know. I thought I heard a struggle before the crash."

Wrigley's face was incredulous. "Drugged? Who would have wanted to drug the pilot?"

Maddie felt a prick of interest. She'd been so focused on the heart, she hadn't had time to think about the pilot's last words. "Someone who wanted my father dead." Her words echoed eerily in the cave.

All three men stared at her. Jaden spoke first. "Who would benefit?"

Maddie took a deep breath. "The hospital. It would be better for them if my father died, rather than continue the financial investigation he started before the crash." She locked eyes on Wrigley. "Because you don't want my father to uncover any irregularities, do you?"

Dr. Wrigley shook his head. "That's preposterous."

"I don't think it's so preposterous. And after the surgery he intended to file a malpractice suit."

Paul jerked. "Malpractice?"

She forced her chin up. "Yes. He believes the children died because the E.R. was understaffed and…"

He stared at her, disbelief strong in his eyes. "And because he thinks I was professionally negligent?"

She didn't answer.

His voice trembled with emotion. "Is that what you think, Maddie? Deep down, do you believe I turned my back on those children, gave them insufficient care and let them die?"

She wanted to glare at him, to feel her father's hatred flow through her, but the anguish in his eyes, the betrayal she saw carved deep in the gray depths, stopped her. Instead, she looked away. "What I believe doesn't matter anymore. We're talking about a motive for crashing the plane. Now that the heart's ruined, it looks like things just got a lot better for Bayview Hospital."

Paul's laugh was bitter. "And for me, too. Maybe I can escape a malpractice suit now. I guess that gives me a pretty good motive for drugging the pilot, if it weren't for the fact that all of us should have been dead from that crash."

She recoiled from the razor edge in his words, wishing she'd kept her mouth shut, but it was too late.

Wrigley stood, good hand on his hip. "I agree with Dr. Ford. I certainly wouldn't have arranged to crash the plane on which I happened to be a passenger. I have no love for Bruce Lambert, but I'm not about to give up my life to punish him."

Jaden held up a hand. "There was another person who didn't make the flight. Someone else who would benefit if the investigations went away."

Wrigley jerked as if he'd been slapped. "Director Stevens?"

Maddie watched him closely. Wrigley finally shook his head. "No. Director Stevens and I have butted heads, but at the end of the day we're both doctors. We got into this business to serve people, and I don't believe he'd sacrifice six lives. He's not a murderer. Do you agree, Paul?"

Paul ran his hands through his hair. "Yesterday, I would

have agreed with you. At this moment—" he looked at Maddie "—I don't trust anything I believed in before."

Maddie felt his gaze burning into her, but she did not look at him.

"It could be," Jaden continued, "that plans were changed at the last minute and all the parties involved were not informed. Perhaps, the copilot was paid to slip drugs to the pilot and land the plane somewhere off-course, to cause delay, or to disappear with the heart."

Maddie noticed how the strange light picked up the silvered strands in Jaden's hair. His face was weathered, tough and grim. "Who would do that?"

"It's entirely possible that Dr. Wrigley or Paul is part of a scheme with the director to see that the heart never reached Bruce Lambert."

"But—" Wrigley began.

"But," Jaden finished, "the plans changed. Perhaps the director decided to switch things up." He looked slowly from Wrigley to Ford. "To take care of anybody who could turn evidence against him later. Or maybe the pilot realized what was happening, fought back and caused the crash."

Wrigley clutched his shoulder and took a step toward Jaden, as if he meant to hit him. "I don't have to listen to this."

"I think you do." Jaden waved a hand around. "You've got nowhere to go, no title to hide behind and no secretary or staff to shield you. Here, your reputation and skills mean nothing. You're just another crash victim, Dr. Wrigley, and you know more about our situation than you're letting on."

Maddie held her breath as Paul's face twisted in anger.

His hands balled into fists as he drew an arm's length from Jaden. "Hold on, Jaden. These are pretty serious accusations."

Jaden nodded. "I know."

"Maybe we should be asking *you* a few questions. You

certainly don't act like some lowly company rep. Dr. Wrigley
worked for months with Heartline, and he never heard of you
before, yet you seem to know a lot about our situation. Who's
to say *you* weren't hired by the director to destroy the heart,
and he turned tables on you?"

Jaden smiled, and there was something in the expression
that told Maddie things were about to change. She watched
in fascination as he reached for his backpack and drew out a
nylon-wrapped package.

"Because of this," he said, holding up the Berlin Heart.

FIVE

Paul found himself speechless, mesmerized by the sight of the pristinely packaged Berlin Heart, the same heart he'd believed buried under a sheaf of burning metal not an hour before. He ripped his eyes away to look at Maddie. Her expression was as incredulous as he felt.

"How...?" she started, taking a faltering step toward Jaden.

Wrigley stared, eyes round and mouth open.

Paul reached out a hand to both steady and stop her. She clung to his arm. "Jaden, you've got some explaining to do. Right here, right now."

Jaden shot a glance at the entrance to the cave. "I'll tell you all about it, but right now we've got other priorities." He bobbed his chin at the piling snow. "We need to keep this clear or we'll be trapped inside here."

Paul stepped closer. "We'll take care of it right after you come clean."

Jaden sighed. "Later."

Paul cut him off. "No. *Now.* You and I went into a burning plane and clawed through that rubble. You were with me the whole time, and I never saw you remove that heart. I think you had it with you since we left San Francisco."

He looked from Paul to Maddie and back again. After a

beat he said, "Yes, I've had it the whole time. Mr. Lambert contacted Heartline and expressed his concern that someone from the hospital might try to tamper with the heart."

Wrigley gasped. "Unbelievable. We broke our backs getting this device for Lambert. We are doctors, not two-bit thugs."

Paul held up a hand. "Let him finish."

"Heartline assigned me to carry the heart and see that it reached its destination safely."

Maddie's face was pale. "So the box on the plane…?"

He shrugged. "Contains a prototype model, not the real thing."

For a moment, the only sound was the wind blowing against the snowbank outside.

Paul tried to keep his voice level. "I don't believe you. I think you found a moment to switch the hearts before the flight took off, for some reason of your own."

Jaden raised an eyebrow. "Like what?"

Wrigley found his voice. "To extort money from Mr. Lambert, perhaps?"

"Good theory, but what about the crash? That would derail any plans to profit from stealing the heart, wouldn't it?"

Paul's mind raced. "The crash surprised all of us, but I still think you're a liar."

Jaden put the pack down on the floor and stood, feet apart, arms at his sides. "It doesn't matter what you think."

Paul didn't miss the body language. If the guy was ready for a fight, he'd give it to him. "I'm not going to let you get away with stealing that heart."

Jaden brought his fists up when Maddie stepped between them. "Stop. Whatever the reason Jaden switched the packages doesn't matter. Don't you see?" She turned burning eyes on Paul. "The important thing is the Berlin Heart is intact. If we can get help, my father doesn't have to die."

Paul saw the desperate hope shining on her face. He looked at Jaden, closed, guarded, and knew that the man was lying. "Maddie…"

"Please, Paul." She put a hand on his chest and its gentle pressure made him dizzy. *Maddie*…he thought. *Maddie, this man is not on our side.* But the emotion in her body, that seemed to radiate from her trembling fingertips straight into his soul, stopped him.

He stared at Jaden. "All right. What we've got to do now is focus on staying alive until help arrives and we can get the heart to Maddie's father." The rest of it—intended for Jaden—remained unspoken. *And I will be watching you every moment until that happens.*

Jaden turned his attention to the approaching storm. "Weather's worsening. Here." He handed Paul a pair of boots. "Found these in the plane. Must have been the pilot's."

Paul reluctantly pulled them on before he turned to Wrigley. "Stay here with Maddie—" he lowered his voice "—and watch that heart." He zipped his jacket. "Jaden and I will see if we can find something to shovel the snow away from the entrance. Can you two organize whatever supplies we've got? Set aside any food items or first-aid materials you can find."

Wrigley bristled. "You don't mean we should go through luggage, do you? That's an invasion of privacy."

Paul checked his temper. "It's between survival and privacy, Dr. Wrigley. Take your pick. Mine is the blue duffel. Feel free to tear it apart."

Wrigley didn't answer, but his cheeks flushed.

Without a word, Jaden put on a cap and followed Paul into the snow.

The afternoon sunlight shone through the clouds, illuminating the ground in a dazzle of white, even as the snow continued to fall. Trying to keep Jaden in his line of sight, Paul approached the still-burning wreckage, looking for pieces of metal that had ripped loose and could be used as a makeshift shovel. Facts whirled through his mind, as snowflakes danced around his face.

If Jaden stole the heart for blackmail purposes, then who drugged the pilot? As much as he didn't want to believe it, Maddie's accusations were beginning to sound more logical. The hospital director asked Wrigley to go in his place. Did he arrange to have the copilot disable the pilot and take them off course? Or perhaps Wrigley had been instructed to disrupt the delivery, unaware that Director Stevens intended to take care of the problem another way?

With a start, he realized he didn't trust any of them. But for the moment, they needed each other. It would take all of them to survive until help arrived. He looked at the sky, thick with snow.

If it arrived.

The transponder in the plane had probably broadcast their position, if it hadn't been completely destroyed in the crash. Or maybe the pilot had managed a Mayday before he became incapacitated. In either event, they'd be on their own for a while.

He thought of Maddie's face again, the hope that shone there as it had before the car accident. The mask of grief had slipped away for a moment, and it took his breath away. He stopped the stream of memories and continued his search.

Jaden yanked at a piece of metal, pulling it from underneath the snow.

Paul retrieved a plastic door, torn loose from some compartment on the plane, and they carried their finds to the cave.

Maddie had sorted what she'd been able to salvage. He saw her bent over his bag, extracting the clothing and folding it into a neat stack. He smiled.

Wrigley was repacking the first-aid kit with all the seriousness he approached a surgery.

Paul readied the door in front of him and began to plow the cave entrance, pushing the snow into piles away from the opening. Jaden did the same with his rescued metal. The snow was heavy and unyielding. Soon Paul found himself beginning to sweat. He removed his jacket. It would be a disaster to dampen his clothes with sweat as the temperature dropped. Wet clothes plus low temperatures were the quick route to hypothermia.

They continued on, and Paul could see Jaden found the work difficult, too, but he didn't complain. Jaden's arms were strong, his shoulders wide and solid. He looked more like a toughened ex-marine than a corporate man. Yet another reason to believe Jaden was not what he appeared to be.

They continued clearing the opening until they were both winded and Paul's ribs burned along with the muscles on his back. Maddie appeared to check over their work. "Why don't you take a break? We've found some food."

"A few more minutes. I want to get a jump on it, since there's more piling up." He turned to start again, and heard Maddie gasp.

Maddie was shocked to see the blood soaking through the back of Paul's shirt. She knew it was from the glass that had cut him when he shielded her. She grasped his arm. "You need to come and sit down. You're back is bleeding."

He gave her an odd look. "I'm okay."

"No, you're not." She pulled him by the wrist back into the cave, and propelled him into a seat on a rock before she went for the first-aid kit from Wrigley. As gently as she could, she pulled up the torn fabric, revealing several shallow cuts and one deep one, parallel to his spine. She squirted some disinfectant onto a pad and began to sponge away the blood.

He jerked at her touch.

"Hurts?"

He shook his head. "Just cold, Nurse."

"Funny." She continued to clean the wound, running the pad of cotton over his hard back. It brought back a memory of a day spent at Half Moon Bay, when Paul had refused her suggestion of sunscreen and burned himself to a fiery tomato-red. She'd smoothed on aloe then, and they'd both laughed at his stubbornness. The wound looked angry and sore, and she felt the urge to stroke her finger across his broad shoulder to draw some of the pain away.

She shook herself back to reality. Circumstances, grim as they were, did not erase any of the horrible trauma that had torn them apart. She covered the wound with gauze, taping it securely into place.

Dr. Wrigley nodded his approval. "That will do until the rescue team arrives."

Maddie handed him the supplies to repack, and eased the tattered shirt over Paul's back.

"Thank you." Paul flexed his arms and she saw the twinge of pain on his face. She felt the intense urge to be somewhere, anywhere away from him. She joined Jaden as he examined the pile of meager supplies, including a small, bright red bag the men had rescued from the cockpit. It contained a minimal survival kit, with a lantern, flashlight, extra batteries, two light sticks, a jug of water, flares, a plastic tarp and a radio. She felt her spirit soar when she took in the radio.

Jaden noticed her look. "Shortwave. Will only work if another is in the vicinity."

She sagged.

Wrigley looked over the collection.

"Six protein bars, three bottles of water and…" He squinted. "Five packages of M&M's?"

She thought Paul's cheeks pinked. "I've got a sweet tooth."

Did he ever. As long as Maddie had known him, he'd always kept a little packet of something sweet concealed in a jacket pocket or the glove box of his car. Once she'd even found candy in his coffee mug.

Dr. Wrigley joined them. "Well, I for one am starving. I skipped breakfast." He reached for a protein bar and then stopped and gave the other three a searching look. "May I?"

Paul said, "We need to eat, but sparingly. In case the rescue is delayed awhile."

Maddie's stomach clenched. "They'll find us soon. Planes have emergency signal boxes, don't they?"

Jaden took a protein bar, tore off a big bite and rewrapped the rest, stowing it in his pocket. "Our plane had an ELT, I'm figuring. That's an emergency locator transmitter. When we disappeared off the radar, it alerted a flight controller that we were in trouble. They'll send out a rescue team, but the weather's bad and we're in a remote location."

Paul pressed a bar into Maddie's hand, along with a water bottle. "Eat some." He took one, too, but did not make a move to unwrap it. He put the remaining food in the red pack.

She managed to take a bite of the bar, which was almost frozen. "Aren't you going to eat?"

"Later."

"What about a fire?" Wrigley said between chews. "Shouldn't we try to get one going?"

Paul gazed up at the ceiling. "Don't think that's a good idea. This place is basically a series of ice tunnels. Any heat might weaken sections. I think we're better off waiting until the snow stops and then we can try to make one outside."

Maddie shot an uneasy glance at the smooth cover above their heads. They couldn't risk a cave-in but she was cold—more than cold, her hands almost numb. She looked at her meager pile of possessions and wished again she'd packed more into her carry-on. Her suitcase hadn't survived the crash.

Paul, true to form, had crammed all his belongings into his duffel. He had three sweatshirts and several long-sleeve flannel shirts, and even swim trunks, as if he'd intended to linger in some Washington hotel, perhaps. Making a vacation out of her father's life-and-death struggle? A jet of anger flamed to life inside her. *Remember why you're here.* After the surgery, her father would do his best to prove malpractice, and Paul would be lucky to work anywhere, if her father's suit prevailed. She watched him pull on two of the flannel shirts over the tattered one he wore, and put his jacket on again. Then he picked up the sweatshirts and handed one to Wrigley.

A funny look crossed Wrigley's face, but he accepted it, quickly taking off his jacket, pulling on the extra layer before scuttling into his jacket again. Paul offered one to Jaden, but he refused.

"I'm good."

They locked eyes and Maddie could see the distrust between the two men. After a moment, Paul brought the remaining shirts to her. "Why don't you put these on?"

"I'm fine."

"No, you're not. Your lips are turning blue."

She bridled. "I said I'm fine. We'll be out of here soon."

"I'm sure. But frostbite might be here sooner."

She glared at him. "I don't want to take anything from you."

He blinked, but did not move. "Maddie, when you do get back to your father, and I'm sure it will be soon, I want you to have all your fingers and toes. I'm sure Bruce would want that, too."

She bit her lip, hating that he was right, and detesting the fact that she needed him for help.

She did not want to need him, ever again.

In spite of the bitter taste in her mouth, she took the sweat-shirts and went to a corner of the cave to remove her jacket and slip them over her silk blouse. Though she would never let him know, the soft material felt as comforting as a blanket in the cruel chill. When she returned to the group, they were putting on as many pairs of socks as they could fit.

"Keep a few pairs in your bag, in case your feet get wet," Paul cautioned.

Wanting to avoid another scene, Maddie grabbed a pair of what turned out to be Jaden's crew socks and put them on. There were not enough gloves to go around, so Wrigley pulled a pair of socks over his hands instead.

They sat together, silent for a moment, until Wrigley spoke.

"I can't bear just sitting here. I'm going to try my phone again." He walked out into the blowing snow. Paul followed him as far as the cave entrance.

Maddie took a swallow of water and watched as Dr. Wrigley staggered onto the brittle surface, pockets of snow collapsing under the weight of his feet. "Are you afraid he'll fall?"

Paul shook his head. "More afraid he'll wander too far away and become disoriented."

Wrigley stopped to peer at his cell, then moved a few paces to the left and tried again.

She heard Paul sigh. "You don't think he's going to get a signal, do you?" she asked.

"Nope, but at least he feels like he's doing something." He jammed his hands into his pockets.

Paul didn't like to lose, and he couldn't tolerate inertia while others succeeded around him. It was the reason he'd finished medical school in record time and volunteered to do every lousy shift during his residency. He was driven to constant action, the relentless need to achieve. It had cost him friends and prior relationships, she knew, but it was the thing that made him a brilliant doctor, or so she'd thought until the day her nieces died.

It had not occurred to her before that sitting in a cave, waiting for rescue, must be like torture for him. He continued to stare out into the blinding white, now illuminated to dazzling perfection by the late-afternoon sun. His eyes were shadowed, face grim. Though she didn't want to have a conversation, something inside made her break the silence. "We're all alive. That's a big thing."

"Not all of us."

She followed his gaze to the small hill where they had left the pilot, feeling suddenly ashamed that she'd dismissed the man from her mind so easily. And the copilot, too. Guilty or not, he was also dead. She'd forgotten about the deaths, but Paul hadn't.

"There was no way to save him," she found herself saying.

He turned to her slowly, his eyes boring into hers. "I always believe there's a way, Mads. And if I don't find it, if I don't save them, they stay in my heart, in my gut, forever."

She opened her mouth but no words came out. It was the truth, she could see it in the emotion that shimmered on his face. Ginny and Beth would always be imprinted on his heart. Was the guilt stamped there, too? The fact that he'd saved his brother and given up on the girls? Finally, she forced in a breath. "My nieces will stay in my heart forever, too, and my father's, and my sister's." She turned to go, but he grabbed her arm, face intense with emotion.

"I know your father thinks I let them die to save Mark, but what do you think? Tell me, Maddie." His fingers tightened. "I want to hear you say it to my face."

She tried to pull away. "Let go."

"Not until you say it. Tell me to my face that you believe I let your nieces die."

His eyes blazed and she could not look away. He moved closer so his face was inches from hers. "Say it, Maddie," he whispered. "If you think I let them die, say the words. You owe me that much."

"Stop it," she breathed. "This isn't the right time to have this conversation."

"When *will* it be the right time?"

"Never. You know how I feel about what happened."

"Then say it."

She felt her mouth trembling and willed herself not to cry. He would not bully her into saying anything. His hands slid up her arms to grip her shoulders, forcing her to look at him.

"Maddie, tell me you believe I gave up on those little girls."

"I…"

Jaden shot to his feet. "Quiet. Listen."

Paul let go of Maddie and she hugged herself, willing her heart to slow so she could hear over the sound of her pounding pulse.

"What is it?" she managed.

The sound of an engine rose over the rush of falling snow.

SIX

Paul reluctantly left Maddie and ran to the mouth of the cave. Dr. Wrigley stood frozen, hand clutching his phone and eyes wide. He'd heard it, too, the noise of an approaching engine. Rescue.

"They found us," he called. "They found us." His jubilant laughter echoed off the side of the mountains. The sun had begun its descent and the area was awash in gray shadow. It was hard to pinpoint from which direction the rescue vehicle approached.

Jaden and Maddie joined Paul and they watched as a snowmobile pulled up on the ridge. Paul allowed the relief to wash through him. They would get out alive, with time to see that the Berlin Heart made it to Bruce Lambert. His strange foreboding that their rescue would not arrive in time hadn't come to pass. He risked a glance at Maddie. She had her hands pressed to her mouth, as if she did not quite believe what she was seeing.

Jaden looked as though he did not quite believe it either, thick eyebrows drawn together. He was carrying his backpack. Paul watched as the snowmobile pulled to a stop along the ridge above them.

Wrigley was moving now, waving his arms wildly at the vehicle, as if he were cheering at a sporting event.

"Here. We're over here," Wrigley yelled.

Through the blinding snow, a figure dismounted, dressed in a thick jacket, ski cap pulled down to his goggle-covered eyes.

Maddie sucked in a breath and started out of the cave as the figure bent to retrieve something from his pack.

Paul wondered why the man did not raise a hand in salute, why there seemed to be no urgency in his movements, no jubilation at discovering the survivors. There was a stiffness to his manner, an odd jerk of his arm as if he'd gotten some snow down his sleeve.

Paul glanced at Jaden, who was staring intently.

Maddie stumbled past him onto the snow and he reached for her. "Hold on a minute, Maddie."

She acted as if she did not hear him, face radiant with the promise of rescue.

Paul squinted at the tree line, looking for a sign of other rescue vehicles approaching, but he saw nothing but miles of undisturbed white.

The man straightened and Paul strained to see through the curtain of snow.

Not taking his gaze off the stranger, Paul put a hand on Maddie's shoulder. "Mads, don't move."

She tried to shake him off. "What are you saying that for? Are you crazy? We're being rescued."

He saw a glint, just a blur of something metallic.

"Here," Wrigley continued to shout. "We're all right here."

Paul had a split second to push Maddie down as the stranger began to fire the rifle.

Wrigley, immobile, stared with stark disbelief on his face.

"Get down," Paul yelled. He sprinted toward Wrigley and tackled him as a shot sizzled over their heads.

"What?" Wrigley stammered. "What is he...?"

Paul had no time to answer as the man took aim again. "Roll!" he shouted, and he and Wrigley moved a fraction of a moment before the next bullet plowed into the snow. Now they were up and running, sprinting toward the cave, bullets punching through the air around them.

Jaden had already gotten Maddie inside when Paul and Wrigley crashed through the opening, losing their footing on the slick floor and falling into a tumble.

Paul scrambled to his feet. "Go into the tunnels. Find somewhere to hide."

Maddie didn't move, her face frozen in shock. Paul shoved her toward a small opening at the back and pushed her in. Wrigley had regained his footing by this time and followed, face as pale as milk. Paul and Jaden brought up the rear, scrambling as far into the dark space as they could, until the low ceiling forced them onto hands and knees. Rocks bit into their knees as they moved in confusion deeper away from the main cave. Wrigley half crawled along, unable to put weight on his wounded shoulder. Their pace slowed, sweat beading on their faces in spite of the bitter cold.

"Where does this lead?" Maddie breathed.

"Just keep going," Jaden said. "As fast as you can."

Paul helped Wrigley over a pile of rock that littered the floor.

Abruptly, the tunnel pinched off. They huddled, panting, eyes glowing white in the near dark. Jaden flicked a lighter and the small blue flame showed the dire truth.

There was nowhere to go, no other passages branched off. They were trapped.

"What's happening?" Maddie whispered.

Paul hated the fear in her words. He forced a calm into his voice that he did not feel. "I don't know, but I'm going to find out. Stay here and don't make any noise to give away your location." He turned to ease around Wrigley and crawl back out the passage.

Maddie clutched his arm. "Where are you going?"

"To try and lead whoever that is away from here."

He heard her breath catch. "He'll kill you."

"Nah," Paul said, wishing he could hug her. "I'm stealthy, remember? Who beat you at paintball every single time?"

Her face didn't lighten. "You're a doctor, not an action hero."

He gave her a wan smile. "I know it, but somehow I can't figure out how to save us by taking that guy's blood pressure, so I'll go for distraction." He tried to see the contours of her face in the gloom. Reaching out he squeezed her gloved fingers. "It will be okay. Stay here."

Maddie opened her mouth but did not speak.

Jaden handed Maddie his backpack and moved to join Paul. "I'll go with you. What's your plan?"

"I'll let you know when I think of one."

Jaden sighed and they moved carefully, trying not to make any noise as they returned through the twisting passage. Paul's hands and knees were raw by the time they reached the main cavern. He stilled his rasping breath as both men paused to listen.

Nothing. No sound except the storm-blown snow from outside.

Jaden put his mouth to Paul's ear. "Do you think he left?"

Paul raised an eyebrow and whispered back. "He didn't seem like the giving-up type to me."

Jaden nodded. "Me neither."

"I don't suppose you have any idea who this is that wants us dead? We can't pin this one on the copilot."

Jaden's mouth quirked, but he shook his head. "No, but it could be someone who was supposed to rendezvous with the copilot. Our only hope is to overpower him somehow, take control of the situation."

Paul hated to admit that Jaden might be right, but it would explain how the shooter found them before the rescuers had. "Yeah. That's the plan I came up with, too, but I was hoping for a better one." They eased out of the tunnel and hid behind the rocks.

Whoever it was wanted them dead, and he had plenty of time to make his way down from the ridge where he'd started the assault. Paul's legs began to ache from his cramped posture, but still he heard no noise to give away the position of the intruder.

"I'm going to make my way closer to the opening."

Jaden gave him a thumbs-up. "I'll cover you."

"With what?"

Jaden held up a baseball-size rock in each hand.

Paul considered the irony as he picked his way along. He was a doctor, trained in the use of lasers and electronic microscopes and all manner of high-tech equipment, and yet he was trapped in a cave with only rocks to defend himself, without even a working cell phone to call for help. *Lord, we're going to need some help here.*

As he moved along, in spite of his best efforts, rock crunched under his feet and he slid a foot or so before regaining his traction.

He thought he heard movement outside and grabbed the nearest rock he could find to hurl at the would-be assassin. There was no time to do so, when a shot exploded into the space and drilled the wall behind his head, showering him with jagged bits.

The sound almost deafened him as he dived, scrambling forward toward the next boulder as the volley of shots continued. Jaden shouted from the other end of the cave and Paul heard the gunman swear as he fired in the other direction, leaving Paul free to lob as many rocks as he could toward the mouth of the cave. He threw blindly, hoping the barrage would at least slow the gunman down long enough for Jaden to find a hiding spot.

Paul's legs trembled as he exposed his torso in order to hurl more rocks. The man was dressed in black, face fully covered by a ski mask, breath coming in puffs through the mouth opening. Heaving the rock in his hand as hard as he was able, he saw it sail through the air and glance off the stranger's head.

The man stiffened and began to fire wildly.

The trembling in Paul's body increased and he realized that it was not his muscles that betrayed him but the cave itself. Tremors shuddered and shook the walls and floor. The massive ice dome above their heads, disturbed by the shooting, was loosening.

"Jaden, it's coming down," Paul shouted, shielding his head from fragments of ice raining from the ceiling. He was not sure if the gunman had sought cover, but he couldn't worry about that when he was about to be crushed under ten tons of glacial ice. Trying to keep behind whatever rocks he could find, Paul staggered back toward the tunnel. He had to get Maddie out, gunman or no gunman.

He saw no sign of Jaden as he careened on. A blur of bright color caught his eye and he snatched up the red bag that held their meager supplies. A sharp crack rumbled through the cave and the shudders increased until Paul could only hurl himself toward the rear wall, rocks tumbling loose around him.

He caught a glimpse of Jaden, arm raised above his head, shouting something which Paul could not decipher.

With a deafening roar, the entrance to the cave began to collapse.

* * *

Maddie felt the tunnel shudder around her. She shouted over the noise. "What is it?"

Wrigley shouted back, the whites of his eyes gleaming in the dark. "Cave-in. We'd better get out of here before we're buried alive."

Maddie didn't argue as she pulled the pack on in front of her to shield it from the cascade of small rocks that trickled down on them with increasing ferocity. She scrambled after Wrigley, making her way back toward the entrance. Blood roared in her ears from the frantic effort. What worried her more than the movement of the earth was the sound of the rifle shots that had come before. Too many of them to count.

What chance had Paul and Jaden against an armed rifleman? She thought she'd heard a shout before the second volley of shots, but she could not tell if it was Jaden or Paul. Swallowing hard, she fought her way forward along the floor, which seemed to move under her like a raft caught in dangerous rapids.

A rock glanced off her temple and she screamed. The pain stopped her, and she wiped away a hot trickle of blood from her face. When she looked up again, Wrigley had moved far ahead, almost disappearing around the turn.

"Dr. Wrigley, wait," she called.

Wrigley didn't slow his pace. She wiped at the blood and hastened to catch up with him, hands sore from constant abrasion, head throbbing from the wound. The shuddering began to ebb as she pressed forward, a weak light promising the end of the tunnel was close. Turning the last corner, she almost plowed into Dr. Wrigley, who had stopped, his gaze fixed on the cavern.

"What?" she whispered, fear rising.

He didn't answer, only crawled out of the tunnel and straightened.

She did the same, unable to suppress the cry which rose to her lips. The mouth of the cavern was obliterated, filled with a massive wall of broken rock and ice where part of the ceiling had collapsed. Wafts of dust and pulverized ice still floated among the rubble.

"We're trapped in here," Wrigley said.

Maddie shifted Jaden's bag to her back and pushed past him. "Paul?" she called.

Wrigley grabbed her arm. "Quiet. The gunman might be in here. You want to get us shot?"

She ripped her arm out of his grasp and picked her way forward. "Paul? Jaden? Can you hear me?" There was an answer from somewhere to her left, but she could not identify the speaker. It was possible it was neither man, but the shooter who beckoned to her.

Would she step forward, only to receive a bullet in her chest? Fear prickled her skin and made her whole body go cold. She tried to draw comfort from winter memories of the past. Her father's big, boisterous laughter when he taught her and Katie to ice skate. Paul's bumbling attempts to stay upright when she'd tried to teach him the same. So many joyful moments. Would all those memories end here? By a man whose name she did not even know?

She gritted her teeth and made her way toward the voice, the rock shifting and sliding under her feet, some surfaces slick with ice. "Paul?" she called again, keeping her volume down as much as she could. "You've got to answer me."

After an eternity, she heard him.

"Mads."

She was never so happy to hear one syllable in her life. Paul was alive. "Thank you," she breathed, wondering who it was she spoke to.

Paul was writhing around when she found him; and at first glance she mistook his movements for pain, until she realized he was trying to free himself from the pile of rubble that entrapped his lower body.

She knelt next to him and used her hands to scoop away the smaller bits. A few rocks were too heavy for her to lift, but she managed to roll them away from Paul's legs until he sat up amidst a shower of debris. She activated her phone to provide a faint light. Paul's face was filthy, and she used her sleeve to wipe the dirt from his eyes.

"Are you okay?"

He coughed and shook more dirt from his hair. "I'm glad to see you, Mads."

She blinked against the tears and gave him a smile. "I thought I told you not to call me Mads."

"I forgot." He tapped a finger to his temple. "Could be a head injury."

"Uh-huh." She looked him over. "Are you okay?"

"As far as I can tell. Whoever was shooting—" Paul stopped to cough again "—caused the entrance to cave in."

Wrigley joined them. "Is he in here with us?"

"I don't think so, but he might be out there, trying to find a way in. Fortunately, the guy's a terrible shot. We gotta look for Jaden."

"No need," said Jaden, stepping forward. His clothes and hair were as badly grimed as Paul's. "I'm here. In one piece, amazingly."

Paul stood with Maddie's help. They looked around the cavern, which now resembled the smoking crater from a bomb explosion.

Maddie saw with dismay that their pile of belongings was now obliterated. The stark facts began to collect in her mind. Wrigley was right. They were trapped. Even if they could somehow dislodge some of the massive pieces clogging the opening, there was a gunman waiting on the other side. "Who is he? Why does he want to kill us?" She didn't realize she'd spoken aloud.

Jaden brushed off his shoulders. "I would put money on it that he was in partnership with the copilot. He's after the heart."

Wrigley snorted. "Right. Well you can't say that crazy person out there is the hospital director. The director is former military, a crack shot. If he'd been aiming for Dr. Ford and Mr. Jaden, they'd both be dead."

Maddie watched Paul's thoughtful expression.

"Stevens wouldn't get his hands dirty," Paul said. "He'd hire someone else to do it."

Wrigley straightened. "That's all very James Bond, but I still don't believe it. Maybe the guy is some deranged hunter type. In any case, it doesn't change the fact that we've got a killer outside and we're stuck in here. Whoever masterminded this thing is irrelevant at the moment."

Maddie had to agree. Their immediate problem was how to stay alive. "We can stay here, hole up until the rescuers arrive. We've got food and…" Her voice trailed off as she eyed the waste that now covered their meager supplies. In addition to their mountain of problems, they now had to add hunger and thirst to the list. She felt like bursting into tears.

Paul rummaged around in the debris by her feet. "I snatched the food bag. It's a little banged up, but at least we've got that."

She was so relieved she threw her arms around him.

Startled, she felt him clutch her instinctively, and he slid his face to the soft part of her neck where he'd so often fit his lips to the spot where her heart beat. Her pulse quickened and she let him go, stepping away so quickly, she would have tumbled backward if Jaden hadn't steadied her. "That's great,

Paul. Quick thinking. We've got a little food and water and I've got the Berlin Heart. All we have to do is wait it out."

When she had the courage to look at Paul, she found him staring at a spot over her shoulder. Wrigley and Jaden did the same, a similar look of horror on both their faces.

She turned to see, almost missing it at first.

Halfway up, the rubble pile trembled slightly. It was a tiny movement that could have been caused by the normal settling of the displaced rock, if it didn't continue on with relentless regularity.

Her heart seemed to stop beating for a moment.

"He's coming for us, isn't he?"

SEVEN

Paul watched the rock shimmy as the man on the other side worked to burrow his way in. It was surreal, stranger than any crazy novel he'd ever read, but his eyes couldn't deny the evidence. The killer was coming in.

He moved back, pulling Maddie with him, toward the far end of the cavern, trying to put together an escape plan. Their only sure avenue was now closed off by ten tons of frozen ice and a guy with a rifle. The tunnel where they'd hidden led only to a dead end.

Wrigley scuttled in front of him and held up a hand. "What are we doing? There's no way out."

Paul saw the fear written in his face and he tamped down his own irritation. "We're going to find another tunnel."

Wrigley looked as though he wanted to argue, but Paul didn't give him the chance. Still holding on to Maddie's hand, he climbed around Wrigley and moved farther into the darkness. Her fingers were tense in his, but she didn't resist.

Clambering over ice chunks, Paul led the way to a giant crevice cracked into the mountain of ice. He stopped, freed the lantern from his pack and shone it into the black abyss.

Wrigley grabbed his arm. "We're not going in there. It could be unstable. It's probably just another dead end."

Jaden shrugged. "There are a dozen tunnels branching off

this main crevice." He pulled off his glove and held up his palm. "The air is cooler and you can feel a slight movement. This opens up to the outside somewhere."

Wrigley fingered his glasses. "But the opening could be small, too small for a person to climb through."

Paul handed the smaller flashlight to Jaden and his own penlight to Maddie. "We've got to take the chance."

"No." Wrigley shook his head violently. "No. I'm not going in there. It's suicide." The lantern light picked up a bead of sweat on his temple.

Maddie held out her hands toward Wrigley, as Paul had seen her do a hundred times with a scared child at the physical therapy clinic. The action moved him. Maddie had no love for Dr. Wrigley. She might even think he was guilty of trying to kill her father; but now, when the man was scared, she reached out in comfort.

"Dr. Wrigley," she said, "we won't have to stay long. As soon as the rescue teams show up, the gunman will take off. They'll be able to get us out of here, but we have to buy some time."

Paul heard the sound of rocks falling back in the cavern they had vacated. The killer was getting closer. "We need to move."

"I'm not doing it." Wrigley's mouth tightened, giving him a ghoulish expression in the lantern light. "I can't. The idea is ludicrous."

Paul's patience unraveled completely. "Okay. You can stay here, but it won't be very much longer before that nutcase breaks through, and I'm not going to stand here and wait to be cut down." He moved forward and, after a moment of hesitation, Maddie followed, Jaden bringing up the rear. Paul heard Wrigley give what sounded like a half sob as he joined the group, and they worked their way past the slick walls.

Relieved, Paul turned his attention to their surroundings.

The crevice was about six feet wide, rising in twisting ripples above them. Though he held up the lantern, it did not illuminate the ceiling of the sprawling canyon. Ahead, he could see only a few feet of space, until the passage twisted and disappeared around a corner. The lantern light drew sparkles from walls, dazzling his eyes until he had to lower it.

Maddie had turned off her small light to preserve the batteries, and she held on to his belt to keep close. He felt anchored, somehow, by the tug of her fingers on his waist. As long as she was alive and the heart was in one piece, there might be a chance.

He moved forward more confidently than he felt. Wrigley was right to some extent. There was absolutely no guarantee that this crevice would lead them anywhere except to a dead end, where they would speedily be located and shot. Jaden came alongside, aiming the flashlight beam into the darkness.

"I'm thinking this was our only option. Do you agree?" he asked.

Jaden didn't look at him. "I didn't see any other tunnel openings. Either there are none, or they were all covered over when the ceiling came down. This is the only choice, unless we'd rather take a stand with the gunman."

"And you still have no idea who the guy is?" He watched Jaden closely.

"Why would you assume I did?"

"Because," Paul said, stepping around a jagged hunk of ice littering the corridor. "You didn't level with us from the start."

Jaden flashed him a close smile. "You have a suspicious mind."

"Funny, how having your plane crash and being shot at will do that."

Jaden pushed ahead, ending the conversation. "I'm going to check out what's past that fissure. Be right back."

Paul thought about the frenzied anger the gunman had displayed when Paul got him with a rock. There was no doubt in his mind they would all be shot, with no special dispensation for a woman. He felt, again, the reassuring pressure of Maddie holding on to him.

She was scared, he knew, desperate to believe they would survive, but he still savored the nearness of her that filled in a part of him that had been missing for what felt like forever.

The slick walls of the cavern grew rough, ribboned with intricate pebbled sections. He drove back the urge to touch the tiny buttons of ice as they passed. Maddie turned on her light and the beam danced off the miniscule facets.

"Amazing," she said.

He noticed how faint her voice sounded. It had been roughly five hours or so since the crash. Hours of stress and constant motion. He pulled her next to him and held the lantern up to see her face.

She looked haggard, eyes shadowed and face pale. Wrigley didn't look much better, his face a mask of concentration as he picked his way along the slippery floor.

"Let's rest for a minute and have some water." He got no resistance from either of them as he unrolled the thin, plastic tarp and insisted they sit. Maddie sank down with a sigh, taking a few swigs of water from her bottle. Paul drank from his and shared it with Wrigley. Instead of joining them, Paul continued on, meeting up with Jaden as he returned.

Half-afraid to ask, Paul did anyway: "What does it look like farther ahead?"

"Good news and bad. Good news is, the passage continues. Bad news is, it looks like there's been some movement of the ice. It's wetter, and more unstable."

Wrigley heard Jaden's last comment as they joined the

others. "Can we go back? Maybe the rescue teams have arrived by now. The gunman could be gone."

As if on cue, they all fell silent, straining to hear any sound of a pursuer. There was only the distant sound of dripping water.

Paul hesitated. His instinct told him to keep going, put as much distance between them and the gunman as possible, but aside from the adventures in his younger days, he was no expert in survival technique. How long could they really afford to keep going, before exposure or injury got the best of them? He felt Maddie watching him and he wished he was more certain about their next move. Jaden flicked on his lighter and moved away from the group. The little flame glowed, making eerie shadows against the frozen backdrop.

"What's he doing?" Wrigley snapped.

Paul noticed the doctor had begun to shiver. Maddie, too. They needed to start moving again. He glanced at Jaden and saw the flame in his hand flicker slightly, wavering to one side. "He's checking to see if there's airflow."

Wrigley capped his water. "Well, is there?"

Jaden nodded, stowing the lighter in his pocket. "Yes. There's an air current. So this tunnel definitely opens to the surface somewhere."

"Somewhere," Wrigley groaned. "I went to the best medical school in the country, and finally got appointed to head of surgery. And here I am, stuck in a tunnel, freezing to death." He turned panicked eyes on them. "We'll die here of exposure, buried under tons of ice. They might never even find our bodies."

"That's not going to happen." He looked at Maddie and found her unaffected by Wrigley's outburst.

"We're going to be okay as long as we keep moving." She stood and pulled on the backpack.

Paul gave her a smile. "If that's getting heavy, I can carry it for you."

She lifted her chin. "No, thanks. I'm not trusting anyone else with this heart until we put it in the hands of my father's surgeon."

Paul turned away to hide his aggravation. It wasn't enough to try to keep her alive, to crawl through frozen tunnels and duck bullets. Nothing he did would ever prove to her that her father was wrong. He'd done everything he could, used every skill at his disposal during those hours. Did she know he still replayed that terrible time, minute by minute in waking nightmares, desperately trying to think of what else he could have done to save them?

No, she didn't know and he hadn't tried to tell her. In her eyes, he'd let them die.

He wanted to kick at a pile of ice. How could she believe it of him? Medicine was his whole life until he met her. Then she became as important to him as his driving need to be the best doctor in the country.

If she was anyone else, he'd let her feelings roll off his back. Families of victims who didn't survive often needed someone to blame, and he did not mind shouldering that burden, because he believed in his own skills. He did not mind, except for this time.

When it was the woman he loved who heaped the blame.

And for all his skills he could not save the two little people who meant the most to her.

Maddie stayed next to Dr. Wrigley as Paul and Jaden went ahead, testing the ice, calling out warnings about loose chunks that threatened to give way. Even so, she found herself slipping often, taking small steps and moving slowly along, the backpack strap clutched in her stiff fingers. Though it could not be as cold in the tunnel as it had been outside, Maddie felt frozen to the core. It was getting difficult not to stumble as she lost feeling in her feet. What she wouldn't give to slide them into a pan of warm water right then.

Not much longer. We'll get to help soon.

The words didn't quite override the doubt deep in the pit of her stomach. Wrigley's fear was rubbing off on her. As she trudged along, she tried to understand how she'd landed in a dark tunnel, half-frozen and, strangely enough, following Paul.

She hadn't thought she'd ever see him again and had tried hard to keep it that way. She could not look at him without remembering them, the girls. The hospital report said they were declared dead first by Dr. Paul Ford, who then focused his attention on his brother, Mark, while another doctor arrived and took charge of Bruce Lambert's case, relieving Dr. Wrigley, who had finally arrived in the E.R.

She knew how much Paul loved his brother. She'd watched him support Mark financially, drive him to Alcoholics Anonymous meetings, pray for his healing and, when he thought his brother was truly sober, loan him a car to drive himself to work.

That car.

The same one that smashed into her father's.

She shook the thought away. *Just keep moving and get the Berlin Heart to Dad.*

When Jaden stopped a few feet ahead of her to again check the air current, she hurried to catch up with him. "I want to ask you something," she said, when he started forward again.

"Shoot."

"You said Heartline asked you to look out for the Berlin Heart because my father contacted them and said he was afraid someone would tamper with it."

"Right."

"Did he give specifics?" She kept her voice low so Wrigley and Paul wouldn't overhear. "Who was he worried about?"

Jaden didn't look at her. "He was investigating Bayview. He claimed someone was trying to dissuade him from doing so."

She nodded. "Did he tell you someone stole his laptop and vandalized his car? He thought it was someone from Bayview trying to scare him off."

He shrugged. "As I said, I don't know the particulars. I just know your father is a real tiger and he gets what he wants."

A tiger? She was so surprised she stopped walking. Tiger was the name Katie's ex-husband had given to her father, and the name had stuck. Even the nieces had called him Grandpa Tiger. Was it coincidence that Jaden picked that term to describe Bruce Lambert? She wanted to stop him, question him and read the truth on his face, but he had moved ahead to speak to Paul.

She and Wrigley caught up and she saw the subject of their discussion. The tunnel branched off into two directions, one leading up and the other more level, but strewn with chunks of ice and rock.

"This one has a stronger current of air," Jaden said, holding his lighter into the sharply sloped tunnel. "Let me see if it narrows over the next few yards."

He and Paul marched into the darkness, leaving Wrigley and Maddie alone. She turned on the light, hoping the thing would generate the slightest bit of warmth. It didn't. She concentrated on listening to any noise that might indicate their pursuer was drawing closer, but she heard nothing at all. She felt an intense urgency to keep moving, to rush as fast as she could through these dark passages. Her father had fluid around both lungs and his belly. A machine was helping him stay alive, forcing his heart and lungs to keep working until the Berlin Heart arrived.

She wished she could call him, tell him she was alive and on her way—anything that would give him the strength to keep going.

Wrigley slouched against the wall, looking ridiculous in his suit pants and parka. She wondered if he still had on his tie underneath all the layers. His eyes darted from ceiling to floor. He looked so small, so powerless in this wild place. Was he really part of a plot to silence her father? Had he been double-crossed by the director?

Her thoughts were interrupted by the sound of footsteps. Jaden and Paul returned, their faces grave.

Paul rubbed his hands together to warm them. "The tunnel looks fairly clear, there's even some snow visible, which means we're getting close to a hole or vent that connects to the outside."

Wrigley straightened. "An exit?"

"Hopefully." Paul frowned.

"So why do you look so worried?"

"Because we're not the only ones crawling around these passages."

She gasped. "The shooter? How would he have gotten ahead of us?"

"Not the shooter. Come on. I'll show you." Paul led them several yards into the tunnel where a fine dusting of snow covered the floor. He aimed the lantern and pointed. "There."

Maddie peered into the gloom and her breath caught.

Pressed delicately into the snow was the imprint of a large paw.

She locked eyes with Paul. "And what kind of animal would make that kind of track?"

He sighed. "Jaden and I agree on this one. It's a mountain lion."

EIGHT

Paul wouldn't have paid a nickel for the movie of their situation. They'd survived a plane crash, eluded a killer, only to run into the lair of a mountain lion? It was too crazy. He watched the horror and disbelief wash over the faces of Maddie and Dr. Wrigley.

"You're joking," Dr. Wrigley half whispered.

Paul had no answer. He could only shake his head.

Wrigley's face was gaunt in the dim light, eyes unnaturally bright, sweeping the small space as if the mountain lion was even now stalking them. Then he began to laugh, a high-pitched, giddy sound that bounced off the walls. He laughed until his face was red and Paul reached out and gripped him by the arm.

Dr. Wrigley tore away and began to kick at the stone. "Everything I've done. Everything I've sacrificed, and it's all going to end here." He slammed his foot viciously into the rock.

Paul tried to pull him back but Dr. Wrigley yanked away, face wild.

Maddie reached out. "Please, Dr. Wrigley. This isn't going to help the situation. You need to calm down."

He spun to face her. "Don't you dare tell me to calm down. This is your father's fault. It was all going fine until he showed up to start poking around. I was head of surgery. Do you hear me? Head of surgery!"

"My father was hired to see if the hospital was being managed well, prior to a possible buyout."

"No," Wrigley spat. "That was an excuse for his real mission. He came in to find dirt on the hospital and me, so he could destroy us. Anything that would smear me, because he's never gotten over what happened with Ellen forty years ago."

Paul saw Maddie's face harden. "You had an affair with a woman who was engaged to my father. Was he supposed to forget that?"

"Your father never forgets anything, and you can call it what you want but he was out to destroy me and Bayview." He shook his head. "Why did I let myself get sucked into this? The whole idea was idiotic, and I knew it from the start."

Maddie's head tilted. "Sucked into what? What are you talking about?"

Wrigley started and turned away. "Never mind. I'm not going into that tunnel to be eaten by a mountain lion. I'll take my chances waiting for the real rescue party." He gave Maddie a final look. "If you can survive this situation, maybe you *are* as tough as your father."

He started back the way they'd come.

Paul tried again. "Dr. Wrigley, there's a man with a gun in that direction."

"At least I'll die quickly." He continued on. Paul had to jog to catch up.

"You could get hurt, lost. Isn't there any way I can change your mind?"

Wrigley looked at him and heaved a sigh. "You're a good doctor, Paul, but know this—the truth doesn't matter to Bruce Lambert. The only thing that does mean anything to him is vengeance. I should have realized that in the first place. If you do get out of this nightmare and keep that old man alive, watch out, because he's coming after you next, and he'll never stop until you're dust under his feet." Wrigley shot a look at Maddie. "His daughter looks like she's turning out the same way."

Paul couldn't think of a thing to say. He stood frozen as Wrigley moved away. Finally his brain kicked in. "Wait." He thrust a bottle of water and the lantern into Wrigley's hands, along with a protein bar. "Be careful, Dr. Wrigley. With any luck, we'll all make it out of here alive."

Wrigley huffed. "I don't have that kind of luck. Not since I tangled with Bruce Lambert." He disappeared into the darkness.

Paul returned to Maddie and Jaden. He wondered what Maddie thought about the outburst. She had no doubt heard Wrigley's parting words to him. Her face looked more troubled than angry.

"What did he mean by getting sucked into an idiotic idea?" she said.

Paul frowned. "I don't know, but the bad blood that runs between him and your father is serious."

She looked at the ground. "My father has reasons for what he does. He isn't motivated by vengeance. He just wants to protect his family."

By destroying other people? Paul kept the thought to himself.

Jaden shrugged. "Wrigley found out what it's like to mess with a tiger. They might take a long time to get you, but sooner or later they will."

Maddie's eyes widened and Paul knew why. He'd heard the nickname before, applied to Bruce Lambert. "So you know her father's nickname. How?"

Jaden shrugged. "It's easy to find out about Mr. Lambert. Google is a wonderful thing."

Maddie rounded on him. "No. You know my father better than you're letting on. Tell me who you really are."

Jaden stared back at them, unflinching. "The only thing I'm going to tell you is, it's in our best interest and the interest of your family to get moving. We're wasting time here and we don't have much to squander."

Paul didn't want to let it go, but he, too, felt the moments slipping by. He held up his illuminated watch. "Almost sunset. If the storm is still active, the rescue efforts might be suspended after dark." He gritted his teeth, picturing Wrigley stumbling along. "It would have been better for us to stick together. He's going to have trouble getting around with a broken clavicle."

"Wrigley's free to make his own decisions, and we've got to do the same." Jaden unwrapped a light stick and activated it. The greenish glow was surprisingly bright in the dark. "Not much, but it's better than nothing. We've only got a flashlight left when we've used the light sticks."

Paul looked again at Maddie. "We can go back. With Wrigley. I'll go with you, if that's what you want."

She stared at the animal prints in the snow. "But we're close. The snow is blowing in from someplace. We're really close, aren't we?"

Paul nodded. "I think so, but it might be too small to squeeze through."

"It's the fastest way out. The fastest way to make it to a place where we can signal a rescue team, isn't it?"

He tried to measure the words. "I believe so, Maddie, but I'm no expert. I'm…" He hated to say it. "I'm not sure what to do here." He'd spent his whole career being sure, cocky, supremely confident in his decision-making, and he wished desperately, at that moment, that he could be sure about this. "I don't want to make the wrong decision for us."

Maddie settled the backpack on her shoulders. "You're

not making any decision for me. I'm making it for myself. Let's go."

Jaden's mouth quirked. "I guess we're moving forward."

Paul sighed, hoping the choice was not going to get them killed.

Maddie had to edge across the snow-dusted floor. Jaden and Paul again moved ahead of her, Jaden lighting the way with the light stick. The passage sloped up and she found herself breathless from the climb. Twisted stalactites stabbed into the darkness, and Paul had to duck his tall frame often, to keep from bashing his head. She did not think it was possible that she could get any colder, but her limbs were in agony, stiff and heavy, resistant to any effort on her part to hurry, in spite of the mounting anxiety in her heart.

Wrigley's outburst had shaken her. More than his hint that he was involved in some kind of plot, was Wrigley's assessment of her father. In Wrigley's mind, Bruce Lambert was a vindictive, unforgiving man.

Could someone really think that about her father? A man she adored? An uneasy feeling danced in her stomach. She had seen her father's relentless side on many occasions, including the nasty episode with her sister's husband, Roger. When Katie discovered a phone message from a woman Roger was having an affair with five years before, Bruce Lambert stepped in and cut Roger out of the family as effectively as a surgeon removes a tumor. No phone calls, no emails, not even Roger's desperate attempts to get onto the Lambert estate did any good. Her father made sure Roger would never hurt his daughter again.

Roger responded by leaving the country after the divorce, and Maddie thought it was the coward's way out. Disgusted as she was by Roger's betrayal, she thought he should have fought harder, hired lawyers to protect his rights to the children. Still, she hoped he'd found a helpful treatment regimen for his Huntington's disease. Maybe someday, when time had healed over the wounds, Katie and Roger could at least be friends again.

Jaden's words echoed in her mind. *Wrigley learned what it's like to mess with a tiger.*

And so had Roger and the plethora of business rivals that Bruce had dismantled over the years.

Maddie often wondered how Roger reacted to the news that Ginny and Beth had been killed. Would he have been able to help Katie deal with the enormous grief that he must share? Unbeknownst to her father, Maddie had a suspicion Katie and Roger had secretly been in contact since the accident, and she decided that might not be a bad thing. Who could understand a mother's loss better than the father?

Paul slipped on the wet floor and narrowly avoided falling. She heard him laugh at his own mishap.

Bruce would not rest until Paul was destroyed, too.

She quickened her pace and tried to move faster, leaving the disturbing thoughts behind in the dark shadows. Ahead, the tunnel narrowed and the three had to squeeze along, sometimes sideways, to continue. The way was precarious, littered with rock and unstable in sections where ice had broken away from the walls and slid into untidy piles. Cold water dripped from the ceiling and Maddie felt a drop slide in an icy trail down her back. She shivered and Paul looked around.

"It's getting lighter. I think we're almost there."

She desperately hoped "there" was a way out of the dark maze. Tripping over an unseen shelf of rock, Maddie fell to her knees. The shock of hitting the cold floor made her cry out. Paul whirled and lifted her in his arms. He felt strong, vital, not anywhere near her own tortured condition. She allowed herself to stay in the circle of his arms until she steadied herself enough to pull away.

"I'm okay."

"Here," Paul said, spreading the tarp out and urging her to sit on a flat rock. "We'll rest for a minute. Have a drink."

She shook her head. The idea of gulping water that was sure to be ice-cold made her quiver.

Paul still held the bottle out to her. "You need to drink."

"No. I'm too cold."

Paul sighed and fished around in his pocket. He held up a crumpled package of M&M's, wiggling his eyebrows. "How about this? It's always a good time for chocolate."

His face was so silly in the middle of their catastrophic circumstances, that she couldn't hide a smile. Holding out her hand, she accepted a few of the candies, as did Jaden. The bits were cold, like round disks of ice, but soon her mouth—which seemed to be the only part of her not completely frozen—melted the candy into a warm puddle of chocolate on her tongue. She ate the rest of them one at a time, savoring the sweet comfort as she never had before.

Though she'd never believed chocolate had a medicinal value, she felt herself buoyed, and even managed a swallow of water. When she tried to replace the cap, it slipped out of her numb fingers and plinked to the ground. Feeling in the darkness, she tried to find the cap.

Her fingers closed around something hard and she yanked it up into the weak gleam from Jaden's light stick. The object was long and white, paler than even the ice walls that surrounded them. Maddie's body tensed as she identified the thing. She screamed, hurling it as far away from her as she could.

Jaden crouched to look closer. He held up the bone for Paul to see. "Rabbit, probably. Left over from the mountain lion's last dinner.

Maddie rubbed her gloves on her pants.

Paul's eyes shifted in thought. "We're almost there. We've

got to just press ahead and hope that, if we do encounter a mountain lion, we're going to be scarier than he is."

Jaden nodded. "I used to live in mountain-lion country. If we run into one, don't run or turn your back. Make yourself look big and threatening."

Maddie wondered if her body would obey that command if the time came. She saw Paul swallow and remove the metal first-aid kit from his pack.

"I figure I can whack it over the head, if nothing else."

Maddie forced a smile. She noticed a dark stain on the back of Paul's jacket. "You need a new bandage on your back."

He shook his head. "It can wait."

"If I have to stop for a snack, you can survive some wound care." He grimaced but turned around, slipped off his jacket and let her tend to the wound. She took the first-aid kit from him, removed her gloves and pulled away the sodden gauze as gently as she could, annoyed that she was taking such pains to care for a person she'd written out of her life.

The gesture was purely humanitarian. She'd have done the same for Wrigley or Jaden.

Paul was very quiet, staring ahead to where Jaden held his lighter up.

She leaned close to whisper in his ear. The faintest scent of soap clung to him, almost undetectable against the smell of burnt plastic from the crash. "What do you think of Jaden?"

Paul jerked as if she'd surprised him, turning to face her as he pulled his shirt back on. "I think he's a liar."

"I agree. He knows more about my father than he's letting on."

Paul covered her hand with his own, and she was too startled at first to pull away. "We're almost through this. As soon as we get out of here, don't let that backpack out of your sight."

She clung to him for a moment, the familiar feel of his skin on hers sending tingles ribboning up her arm. She wanted to press his palm to her cheek, to warm the fingers into suppleness again. His eyes were dark and dull with fatigue when she finally pulled away.

Busying herself putting on her gloves again, she didn't look at Paul until they were once again moving forward. The walls glistened with moisture, and she thought the air was slightly warmer. A chunk of ice came loose and slid in front of them.

"Must be a vent somewhere. A place where volcanic gases escape from below and the ice is thinning."

"I'll take any warmth I can get," Maddie said, placing her feet with care.

Jaden grunted. "Not good. Makes things more unstable. We need to be careful."

As if they hadn't been careful since they started down this terrible path? Maddie shut down the negative thinking. Only a little while longer and they'd be out. She did not allow herself to consider what might lie beyond their frozen tomb.

There was definitely a distinct lightening, the blackness shifting to gray. In spite of her discomfort, the light gave Maddie a spurt of energy. All three of them seemed to move along faster, pushing with increasing urgency toward the light.

Maddie followed the men as fast as she could, rounding one corner after another, skirting puddles of frigid water. When Paul and Jaden stopped without warning, Maddie plowed into Paul from behind. He gasped as she smacked into his torn back.

"Sorry," she mumbled. "Why did you stop?"

He looked at her, his face pale, and moved so she could see. The tunnel pinched closed, swallowing up any chance of further advancement. Her gaze shifted upward to the source of the light. Twenty feet above them was an opening about four feet wide. A pale luminescence that she finally identified as moonlight tumbled down on them with silvery fingers.

She gaped. "*That's* the way out?"

Jaden laughed, but there was no humor in the sound. "Nothing has been easy so far, so why should this part be?" He looked closely at the walls, testing the rock with his fingers. "We're going to have to climb. There are enough places to get a grip, if the rock holds."

"It must be strong enough to hold a mountain lion," Paul said.

"Right. That's one hundred and thirty pounds of agile cat." Jaden looked them over. "Not to be rude, but we're all far from agile at this point."

Maddie knew he was right, but she would not be discouraged when they were so close. "We'll be careful. Go one at a time. I'll go first."

Paul shook his head. "I'll go first. I can pick out the best handholds and show you."

She bridled. "When did you become a rock-climbing expert?"

He flashed her an arrogant smile. "I read about it in a book once. How hard could it be?" He zipped up his jacket and put a foot on the first flat protrusion, pulling himself up. It must have hurt, possibly torn open the wounds on his back again, but he moved doggedly, inching along the rock until he was several feet up.

Maddie took off her gloves and made sure the backpack was snug before she followed. The rocks were slippery and her numb fingers a hindrance. Still, she managed to make her way along. Jaden waited until she was about halfway up before he began his climb.

Maddie concentrated every ounce of strength on pulling herself along the route Paul took as he ascended. Her feet were so cold that she could not always feel the stone under them. A rock broke away from under her hand and she scrambled to find another.

"You okay?" yelled Paul from above.

Her hand found another precarious grip. "Yes," she panted. "How much farther?"

"Only about ten feet. Easy stuff."

She didn't have the breath to offer a retort. A noise like the crack of a whip rang out, and all at once bits of rock and ice were raining down.

"Hold on," Paul shouted.

She clung to the wall, something sharp pressing against her face. Fragments struck her head and shoulders, making her fight to keep her grip. Still, the debris continued to fall.

"The whole thing is collapsing," she heard Paul yell. "We've got to get out. Climb as fast as you can."

Maddie forced her arms to reach through the storm of rock to another handhold. Blindly, she pushed her way up, heedless of the shards that delivered stinging cuts to her face. Her only guide was the sliver of moonlight and Paul's voice shouting something which she could not hear over the roar of falling ice.

She did not know how far she had climbed when the surface underneath her gave way, and she felt herself sliding, falling into the darkness.

NINE

Paul saw Maddie's face raised in terror. Her scream mingled with the sound of falling earth. He reached down and grabbed at her, catching hold of the strap on her backpack. It was all he could do to keep his grip, her weight pulling them both down. He snagged his foot on a twisted root at the mouth of the hole and reached down with both hands. All he could see was the glimmer of her eyes, wide and terrified, as she reached up to cling to him.

Help me hold on, Lord. Give me the strength.

Their hands twisted together, and he knew he did not have the angle or the leverage to sustain the effort much longer. Wriggling backward, ignoring the stab of pain as the lacerations on his back tore open, he pulled her up a fraction of an inch at a time. Snow pushed under his jacket and into his sleeves, but he continued to wriggle back, sweat pouring down his face. He wanted to call some reassurance to her, but he couldn't spare the breath.

Finally, when he thought the muscles in his arms were about to snap, the pressure eased. Maddie moved upward on her own and crawled out next to him. They fell together, panting on the snow. She laid her head on his chest and for a moment there was nothing to be done but breathe. Paul offered up a heartfelt, silent prayer of thanks. They had survived another leg in this terrible journey. His arms came around her and he relished every gasping breath she took.

Her hand found his neck and she clung to him and he to her, for a moment savoring the sensation of life and how close they had come to losing it.

Jaden scrambled up next, and Paul realized he must have been able to push Maddie up from below. His nose was bloody as he crouched next to them.

"Everyone okay?"

Paul reluctantly let her go and sat up, Maddie with him. She took off the backpack and hastily unzipped it. By the moonlight, she examined the package with a look of trepidation.

Jaden patted her shoulder. "It's protected by a layer of insulating material and hard-fused nylon packing. That little avalanche didn't make a dent."

Paul saw her exhale and carefully zip up the backpack. She looked away from Paul to Jaden "Um...thank you. I—I'm sure I wouldn't have gotten out of there without both of you."

He wondered why Maddie would not look at him. Was it so awful to acknowledge that he'd helped her? That maybe he wasn't the callous miscreant her father had convinced her he was? He brushed away the dirt from her shoulder. "Are you okay?"

"Yes, I'm fine." She struggled to her feet and looked around. "But where in the world are we?"

He got to his feet. They'd emerged in a thick wood that butted up to the mountain, massive trunks rising around them. The moon provided enough light for him to see that there was no sign of the wreckage.

"We must have come out on the other side of the mountain." He frowned. "That's good and bad. On the one hand, we might have eluded the shooter."

Maddie eyed the snow-covered slopes. "And the bad news is that we're still lost in the mountains."

Jaden checked his watch. "It's close to midnight. We can't do anything about rescue tonight. We've got to get to shelter." He pointed to the top of the slope. "Let's climb there and identify our best option." He eyed Maddie. "Are you strong enough to make it? I can go and come back with a report."

"I'm strong enough."

Paul hid a smile. She was the strongest woman he knew.

Jaden held out a hand. "Why don't you let me carry the backpack for a while?"

Maddie shook her head. "No, thank you." She began to head up the slope, walking awkwardly in the deep snow.

In spite of her bravado, Paul could see that exhaustion was beginning to take its toll. She was probably dehydrated, too, and on the verge of hypothermia. The temperature would continue to drop, and, if they didn't find some sort of shelter, things would get a lot worse. He quickened his pace until he'd passed Maddie and made his way to the crest.

Looking down, he saw an undulating palette of snow-covered slopes stretching away in all directions. About a half mile down, in a relatively flat area, something caught his eye. He blinked and rubbed a hand over his face to make sure he wasn't hallucinating. When Jaden stopped next to him and let out a slow whistle, Paul knew he wasn't imagining it.

Maddie drew up, panting. "Are those…buildings?"

"Not really," Paul said. "If memory serves, I spent a few long weeks of summer camp in those type of things. They're really just platforms with canvas shells over the top. This must have been some sort of scout camp at one time." He counted four of the structures, the raised platforms keeping them above the snow.

Maddie looked doubtful. "They look like they've been abandoned for a while."

"Now is the perfect time to put them to use." He moved as quickly as he could downslope, hoping the makeshift cabins were in good enough shape to provide them some shelter until morning. The first one he reached was not encouraging. A portion of the canvas roof had been torn away and the inside was packed tightly with snow. The cabin itself was shaky on its raised foundation. He moved on to the second one. The roof was intact. He wrestled with the door and finally pushed his way in. Snow had filtered in through a hole in one corner, and the floor was speckled with animal droppings. On each side of the room were little cots, most moldy and decaying. He poked at the most promising one. It was relatively unscathed by critters and moisture.

It wasn't pretty or even comfortable, as the temperature inside was bone-chilling, but it would give Maddie a place to rest and stay protected from the snow until morning. He flung his arm out. "Welcome to Maddie's château," he said.

He did not know exactly why her eyes filled with tears at that moment, but she ducked her head and meekly shuffled in. "I wasn't a Girl Scout, but I guess it's never too late to give it a try."

He and Jaden left her to check out the other two cabins. One was ruined, but the other serviceable, if they pushed one of the cots against the wall to seal a tear in its side.

"Home, sweet home," Jaden said.

Paul prowled through the space, looking for something they could use to stay warm. There were no blankets or bedding. The place was bare except for the cots. He went back outside and surveyed the landscape with the lantern. Snow covered every surface, smooth and glittering, offering no resources to warm them.

A spark of an idea lit his half-frozen mind, and he pushed through the snow to the dilapidated cabin they'd rejected moments before. He leaned against it, throwing his weight against the canvas wall where it was attached to a sturdy

two-by-four. It gave, just enough. His adrenaline surged as
he threw his weight against it again.

Jaden joined him. "I assume this isn't an act of frustration?"

"If we can get this cabin off its foundation, there should
be an area clear of snow. We can build a fire."

Jaden stared. "No way. You light a fire, you might as well
tell the gunman where to find us."

"He's on the other side of the mountain."

"That's where he was six hours ago. Doesn't mean he's
still there."

Paul stopped pushing. "The way I see it, if we don't get
some warmth soon, we could be dead by morning, gunman
or no gunman, and if there's any smoke visible long distance,
it will help the rescue crew find us."

"I think you're making a mistake."

He fisted his hands. "I don't care what you think. I'm not
going to let Maddie die. She's already close to exhaustion and
risking exposure."

Jaden watched him a moment longer and a shadow of a
grin quirked his mouth. "You still love her, never mind the
fact that her father will destroy you."

Paul sighed, feeling his face flush warm in spite of the
freezing temperatures. "I'm just trying to keep us all alive."

"Sure," Jaden said. "I think you're wrong, but then again,
I'm not a doctor."

Paul heard the tiny stroke of sarcasm in Jaden's voice as
the man took up a position against the opposite corner. On the
count of three, they pushed and heaved until the cabin broke
loose from its foundation and skidded sideways, sinking into
the snow. Underneath, as Paul had hoped, was an exposed
area about six feet square that shone dark with old matted
pine needles and semidry leaves, which Paul scooped into
a pile.

Jaden used his lighter to ignite some of the pine needles. They flamed encouragingly for a moment and then died away.

"Try again," Paul said through teeth gritted to keep them from chattering.

Jaden did, and once again the pine needles refused to catch for more than a moment.

Paul grabbed a strip of the canvas from the broken frame and ripped it loose. He dragged it to the fire. "Maybe this will burn."

Jaden shook his head. "Probably fire retardant–treated."

Paul jammed his hands in his pockets. How could they be so close to a source of heat and not be able to manage the thing? His fingers closed around the crumpled candy bag. He pulled it out triumphantly and laid it with care next to the needles.

Jaden applied the flame and slowly the needles caught, then the candy bag. Paul fed the driest leaves into the flame one at a time, until they caught and ignited a few tiny twigs in the stack. When the flame was steady enough to survive for a few moments, Paul set to work prying up floorboards from the wrecked cabin. Several were already broken, and it was only a matter of effort to muscle the fragments from their nails.

He eased the first onto the burning pile and continued to add leaves and needles as Jaden blew on the mound. After what seemed like an eternity, a small fire blazed in front of them.

"Thank You, Lord," Paul breathed.

"I just hope you're going to be so pleased with yourself when the shooter finds us."

Paul turned away toward Maddie's cabin. "That's not going to happen."

"We'll see," Jaden said. "We'll see."

* * *

Maddie sat on the cot, arms wrapped around herself, too cold and stiff even to take off the backpack. Though moonlight shone behind the canvas walls, the cabin was dark and still, except for the faint rustling of some small thing that burrowed below the raised floor. Her body shivered and she knew she should get up and move around, but her limbs felt frozen in place.

Thoughts flooded into her mind, thoughts she'd suppressed during their crazed escape. Her father might die, might already be dead, and if they didn't find help soon, she would be, too. The horrible choking feeling rose again, just as it had the day she'd learned her nieces hadn't made it. She could only identify it as fear, terror that life—any life, hers included—could stop so abruptly and leave not a shred of comfort behind.

She'd spent the past year willing her father to live, going with him to doctor after doctor, following every detail of Bayview Hospital's efforts to secure the Berlin Heart. She was going to save her father, and until she found herself alone in a dilapidated cabin, she was sure she could do it.

The darkness closed around her and seemed to push inside, chilling her to the bone. After the funeral, she'd developed the strange need to sleep with the lamp on. Now she felt a hysteria building low in her gut. She knew if she didn't get some light soon, the fear would take over and she would go mad. Fumbling in her pocket, she pulled out the flashlight and flicked the switch. It glowed for a moment and then went dark. She shook it but it didn't work.

Pounding it on the bed frame, she felt hot tears trickle down her face. "Work, you stupid flashlight. Work. Don't leave me here in the dark." The trickle of tears turned into gushes that soaked her face and swelled her eyes. Still, she continued to bang the light against the cot until a pair of hands took firm hold of her own.

She looked up to find Paul kneeling next to her, his fingers prying the flashlight from hers. "It's okay, Maddie." He pulled out the last remaining light stick. "You can use this one."

She held it to her chest. *I don't need it. I can handle the dark. I'm not afraid.* She wanted the words to come out but they would not. Paul watched her, and she felt as if he could read her thoughts, see the wild fear that coursed through her underneath the bravado. Not daring to look at him, she swiped a sleeve over her eyes. "Thanks."

"Come with me. I made a fire. It's not much, but it will help."

Fire? There was a chance of warmth, no matter how faint in this frozen nowhere? She hung on to the word as if the letters themselves could bring feeling back into her body. Fire. In a fog, she felt Paul take her hand and lead her out the door. She saw it right away, the flicker of precious orange and yellow, Jaden crouched near, feeding clumps of needles into the flames.

It was all she could do to keep from thrusting her gloved hands into the flames. Paul dragged a cot from the toppled structure and pulled it close. He pushed Maddie onto the cushion.

She held her hands up and inclined her toes toward the warmth. It took several minutes for the heat to penetrate the layers, but finally there was the amazing sensation of thawing, a prickling feeling that turned into pain for a few moments and then blissful comfort. Tears threatened again, and she could not speak for a while. She knew both men watched her and probably thought she was losing her mind, but all she could focus on was the pleasure of that warmth.

When she finally did manage to look up, she noted the worry on Paul's face. Jaden drifted away into the darkness.

"Where is he going?"

"Guard duty." Paul shifted uneasily. "Maddie, I took a risk lighting this fire. Jaden thinks it will alert the shooter to our location."

She started. The cold had forced everything else from her mind. "Do you think he's right?"

He shrugged. "Maybe, but I didn't think there was much choice. It wasn't safe for you to get any colder."

There was such a tender look in his eyes, mixed with worry and pain, that she could not stand it. She looked instead into the dancing flames. "I'm not sure if it was the right thing to do or not, Paul." The heat seemed to thaw something in her heart, which caused her to add, "But I feel, somehow, like it might have saved my life."

He sighed and moved closer, rubbing his hands together. "Jaden and I will take turns on watch while you sleep. You'll be safe in your cabin."

"I don't want to move away from this fire, ever."

"But you're exhausted. As soon as you're good and warm, you should try to sleep."

"Don't you ever get tired of giving medical advice?"

His laugh was low. "You know something? I never do." Something crept into his gaze and the laughter left his face. Was he thinking about the malpractice suit? How her father would not rest until Paul was barred from medicine permanently?

She swallowed. And how Maddie would help her father every step of his vengeful way? She picked up a clump of pine needles and fed them into the fire. Paul sat on the other end of the cot and fished a bag of M&M's from his pocket. He poured some out and offered them to her. She didn't have the energy to protest. She stripped off her glove and took them, pleased to feel the warmth of his fingers when he touched her palm. So many times those hands had stroked her cheeks, guided her over jagged rocks at the tide pools, wiped away the tears of frustration when her patients quit on their therapy, rather than face the pain. So many tender memories in his touch.

She felt a flood of anguish that he could no longer be a source of comfort to her. He'd walled himself away in the weeks following the crash.

No. That wasn't quite true. There had been a stammered attempt at conversation, his stricken face, ghastly white, staring at her in the cheerless emergency-room corridor. He'd tried to tell her, tried to put words to his failure, but she hadn't allowed it.

He'd let them die.

The great Dr. Ford, arrogant, confident, competent.

He'd let them die.

He'd enabled his alcoholic brother.

He provided the very vehicle which Mark Ford had slammed into her precious family.

Yes, he'd walled himself away, and she'd handed him the bricks.

Looking at him now, his eyes painted by firelight and memories, was too hard. She turned away, busying herself tending the little fire. "Do you think the rescue team has arrived yet?"

He sat back as if the spell was broken, his expression and tone businesslike. "Probably at first light."

"How will we get to them?"

"When the sun rises we'll have a better sense of where we are, where we need to head to reach them." His eyes wandered over the mounded snow.

"What are you thinking?"

"I was wondering what happened to Dr. Wrigley. He should have stayed with us."

She shrugged. "He seems pretty good at taking care of number one."

Paul got up and trudged away, his feet breaking through the crusted snow. Maddie wasn't sure if he was looking at something or trying to put some distance between them. Wrigley was his boss and had his own part in the failure to save the children. It was, no doubt, an unfortunate coincidence that kept one doctor stuck in a malfunctioning elevator and the other doubled over from food poisoning, but the ultimate responsibility for the emergency room was Dr. Wrigley's. He'd shown up and tended to her father until another doctor arrived, leaving Paul to handle the rest.

Maddie supposed she should be grateful on some level that Dr. Wrigley hadn't given up on her father and let him die along with the children. Paul might believe Wrigley was a noble figure, but she did not. The hatred in his eyes when he spoke of her father convinced her.

He's coming after you next, and he'll never stop until you're dust under his feet.

She'd seen her father in action, and he was every bit as relentless as Wrigley said, but he'd always had good motives. An unpleasant feeling made her shift on the mattress as she remembered the rest of his warning to Paul.

His daughter looks like she's turning out the same way.

Jaden returned and Paul joined them. They warmed their hands at the fire. "All's quiet, as far as I can tell. No sign of people, but more bad news."

Paul looked at him sharply. "You saw it, too?"

Maddie stared in the direction Paul had been examining. "Let me guess. Animal visitors?"

"Yes." Jaden pointed to the trunk of a tree that was scarred and torn. "Someone has been marking their territory."

She swallowed. "The mountain lion?"

"Yes. It's sort of a 'no trespassing' sign."

She tried to keep the fear out of her voice. "Will the fire keep it away?"

"Maybe, but they're not usually scared of much."

Paul kicked at a pile of snow. "If we just had a gun or a club of some sort."

"Probably wouldn't help anyway."

They both looked at him. Paul spoke first. "Why?"

"Mountain lions aren't going to let you know they're coming. They're masters of the ambush."

Ambush.

Maddie felt the darkness closing in around her and the hair at the nape of her neck prickled. She stared into the blackness, trees casting eerie shadows, twigs crackling in the slight wind. For the first time in her life, she felt what it was like to be the prey—on the run and desperate.

There were two predators out there in the darkness, waiting for them to let down their guard.

Waiting for their moment to ambush.

TEN

Paul's body ached with fatigue, but he could not relax enough to sleep. It was Jaden's watch, but Paul wasn't able to shake the feeling that the man was not who he professed to be. No matter how he thought the thing through, Jaden did not fit into the puzzle. At least Maddie was safe, temporarily, anyway, warmed enough by the fire to get through the bitter hours before dawn. He squinted at the illuminated face of his watch. A few minutes past four. Sunrise would be here soon, and they could start the treacherous hike back to the crash site. It seemed the only option, since they had no idea where they were.

He finally gave up on sleep and returned to the fire to stoke the burning embers into life, adding pine needles and another fragment of wood. There was no sound from Maddie's cabin. A small spot of light showed that she'd activated the light stick. It would not help her through another night, but at least it might have provided enough comfort for her to sleep.

He prayed again for her safety, for God to take away the awful fear that he'd seen in her face earlier. The only antidote to that kind of terror was faith, and Maddie's had been crushed by the accident. He grimaced. Crushed by him.

He held his hands to the fire, feeling the scrapes and cuts more than seeing them.

When things were good, he felt as though there was nothing he couldn't accomplish with his own two hands, no one he couldn't save.

He'd been cured of his pride at a terrible cost.

In truth, the lesson began earlier, the moment his brother, Mark, moved to San Francisco. Every day for two long years, Paul had fought a battle against the addiction that had a firm hold on his brother—driving him to meetings, consulting doctors about his alcoholism; at one point, physically carrying him into a rehab facility.

In his arrogance, he thought he'd won when Mark stayed sober for six months, got a job at the local coffee shop, returning to his old, easygoing self.

"I've got the monkey by the tail now, Pauley."

He'd wanted to believe it so badly, to know that his big brother, the one who'd literally saved his life, was going to win the battle with alcohol. So, when he'd called that morning, pleading with Paul to loan him the car so he could get to work, Paul had allowed it.

He felt the pain sharp and lacerating again. He'd allowed it. And Mark had driven to the liquor store shortly before he plowed into Lambert's car.

Mark's desperate voice rose in his memory. "There was another car. It forced me to crash."

But the police had found nothing, and deep down, Paul knew they wouldn't, because the fault, the real person responsible, was himself.

He'd believed in his own arrogance, that he'd forced his brother to get clean.

How wrong he'd been. How completely and utterly wrong.

Memories flooded his eyes, flashes of the injured children, his feverish attempts to resuscitate them.

"Nothing, Dr. Ford," said the nurse with tears in her eyes. "No heartbeats."

No heartbeats, though he'd tried everything, every trick, every method in all his years in the E.R. No heartbeats. Nothing.

Had he called it too soon? Had he given up one precious moment before his efforts would have made a difference? No. He'd done everything he could.

Would a court of law agree with him, once the influential Bruce Lambert pushed his lawsuit?

With a start, Paul realized he didn't care. The only person he desperately wanted to believe him was the woman lying in the cabin, and she'd made it clear she believed only her father.

When Dr. Wrigley asked him to take a leave, to "let things settle down" after the accident, Paul knew he'd lost everything: his brother in prison; his career, the passion he lived for every day and Maddie.

Maddie.

He'd thought losing those children was the hardest thing he'd ever dealt with, but he was wrong.

It was her condemnation.

He tried to think of something else. The stars above were brilliant where they were not cloaked by clouds. Maybe the North Star would give him some sort of direction as to which way to proceed in the morning. Try as he might, he could not find it.

He was about to feed more needles into the fire, when he heard a whimper coming from Maddie's cabin. Jerking to his feet, he froze until he heard it again, a soft sob, the kind a child might make. She was dreaming, probably in the grip of some nightmare.

It couldn't be worse than the nightmare they were living in the waking hours.

He stood uncertainly, hoping she'd fall back into a more peaceful rest.

Instead, her cries grew louder and he could hear her thrashing around on the small cot.

He took a step toward her cabin, then stopped. She didn't want comfort or anything else from him.

There was the sound of sniffles and a small scream.

His feet seemed to act of their own accord, and he was bounding up the steps and knocking on the splintered door frame. She answered with another cry and he flung the door open and ran to her. She was sitting up, eyes round in the dark, her mouth open and tears dripping down her face.

He knelt next to her and grabbed her hand, squeezing hard. "It's okay. Just a nightmare."

She gulped in air and clutched at his fingers. "Are you... are you sure?" she whispered.

"Yes. You're here in the cabin and you're safe."

She looked wildly around. He guessed the source of her terror, and grabbed the backpack from the foot of the bed, putting it in her lap.

"I dreamed...I dreamed that Dad was dead. I was too late. I ran and ran and ran, but I never could get close enough to hand it to him. I was too late." A new shower of tears rained down her cheeks.

He wiped them away with his palm, her skin satin to his touch. "Mads, we're going to get it there. In the morning we'll find the rescue team and they'll get us to your father."

She took an unsteady breath. "What if we're too late? What if...?"

What if Bruce Lambert was already dead? Then the last piece of Maddie's world would fracture into unmendable pieces.

He gripped her shoulders and willed a confidence into his voice. "We'll get it there in time, Mads."

Her lips trembled and she looked like a lost little girl. "Promise?" she whispered.

"I promise." He said a silent prayer that the Lord would help him make good on his word. He couldn't help himself. He pressed his mouth to hers to kiss away the fear. He tasted the salt of her tears and the terrible fear as she relaxed into him for a moment. Though he wanted to lose himself in the pleasure of having her close, to push away all the pain that severed their connection, he knew she was scared and worn down, vulnerable. He pulled away. "You're freezing. Come warm up by the fire for a while before you go back to sleep."

He waited, trying to stop the whirling in his head from the kiss, while she put on the backpack. He didn't offer to carry it this time. If she needed that to feel in control, as if she was still on track to save her father, then he'd let her have it.

She sat on the cot while he pushed more fuel into the fire. The sky was still black and their breath shone in light puffs in the gloom.

Maddie held her hands close to the fire. "I've never been so cold in my life."

"I guess the winter Yosemite trip is out of the question." He felt his stomach fall to his knees. The joke had come out before he'd thought about it. Their honeymoon trip. Their future. *Stupid jerk,* he chided himself. "Sorry. That was a dumb thing to say."

She looked at her lap. "Do you still think about that?"

"Every day." He tried to catch her eye, but she didn't look up. "Do you?"

There was a pause. She spoke softly. "Every day I remember all the things I've lost."

He'd thought he couldn't feel pain anymore, that the nerves that carried the impulse to grief had been fused hard and useless in the past year. He was wrong again.

The conversation died away, absorbed by the crack of the fire and wind-scuttled branches. She leaned forward on the cot and he thought she meant to go back to the cabin, when a figure hurtled out of the darkness and fell at their feet.

Maddie cried out and knelt by Jaden, heart in her throat. "What happened?"

"I fell. Tumbled down a slope and twisted my ankle. Might be broken."

"Let me take a look." Paul reached for Jaden's pant leg but Jaden shook him off, staggering to his feet.

"No time. Gotta move."

Maddie reached out to stop him when he began to shove armfuls of snow onto the fire. "What are you doing?" The thought of burying that precious warmth nearly drove her crazy.

He continued, talking over his shoulder. "Snowmobile. Heard the engine. Probably a half mile away headed in this direction. He must have heard the sound of the tunnel collapsing when we made it out and located us."

Maddie's breath seemed to crystallize in her lungs. "He found us."

"Not yet," Paul said.

Jaden fell to one knee and got up again. "As soon as he tops the rise, he'll spot these cabins and head here."

Maddie grabbed the backpack. "We'll have to run for it."

Paul stopped shoveling snow. "No. It won't work, not with all of us exhausted and Jaden hurt."

Maddie searched desperately for somewhere, anywhere they could hide. They could probably manage under cover of darkness, but when the sun came up they'd be easy prey. "We'll move as far as we can while it's still dark." She pointed to a bowl-shaped depression several miles downslope, where the trees grew thickly. "There. He can't take his snowmobile there. We can hide."

Paul agreed, but there was a hesitation in his voice. "You and Jaden go."

She stared at him. "And what about you?"

"I'm going to draw him away."

Maddie's mouth opened. "That's crazy." She could only watch as he retrieved the red supply bag from the cabin and shoveled out the remaining protein bars, candy and water, urging Maddie and Jaden to stow them in their pockets. He tore a strip of canvas from the ruined cabin and rolled it into a cylinder, stuffing it into the pack. She finally broke out of her stupor and grabbed his arm. "Paul, what are you doing?"

"I'm hoping he'll think I've got the heart in this bag. I'm going to head back toward the crash site if I can find it. You've still got the shortwave radio so you'll hear if the rescuers show up. Don't talk on it unless you're sure it's for real. The shooter may have a shortwave radio, too."

"But, Paul…"

He shouldered the backpack. "Try to keep to the trees, it will minimize your tracks."

She felt a rising sense of desperation. "This is not going to work. We should stay together."

Paul's expression was all business, as she'd seen it before, the moment a trauma victim rolled through the emergency-room doors. "If we stay together, he'll kill us all."

Jaden nodded but didn't speak.

"Mads," Paul said, holding out his hand. "I'm sorry, but I'm going to have to ask you for the light stick. I'm hoping it's still got a little juice."

Dumbly, she handed it over, the realization dawning on her. "You're…you're hoping he'll follow the light and come after you."

He didn't answer, so she grabbed his arms, her muscles taut as wire. "Paul…"

His eyes glimmered in the moonlight, face full of some emotion she couldn't name.

"What is it?"

What could she say? What words could match the tumble of feelings inside her, the fear that clawed at her insides, the crazy sensation she'd felt when he'd kissed her in the cabin? She could not endure the uncertainty for another second. Instead, she pressed her face to his open palm, feeling the warmth of her own breath against his skin. He put his other hand on the top of her head and stroked her hair gently.

"I'll get help," he whispered, his lips pressed to her hair. She looked up and kissed him quickly on the mouth.

He stared at her for a moment and then pulled her back to him, covering her mouth with his, his lips moving over hers with an intensity she could feel down to her toes.

You're not together anymore, her brain said. *He let you down, he let your nieces die,* but her body did not listen. She found herself lost to everything but the feel of his mouth on hers, the warmth that enveloped her in dizzying sensation. *Paul, don't leave me.*

It was as if he heard the unspoken plea of her heart. "I'll come back," he whispered, his mouth still tracing sparks across her face. "That's a promise."

He gave her cheek another caress before he turned to Jaden, his voice low and full of menace. "I don't know who you are, and I don't trust you. But since we've got no other choice, Maddie's going to stay with you." He leaned close until his face was inches from Jaden's. "If you betray her in

Dear Reader,

We hope you've enjoyed
reading this riveting romantic
suspense novel. If you would
like to receive more of these
great stories delivered directly
to your door, we're offering
to send you <u>two more</u> of the
books you love so much, **plus**
two exciting Mystery gifts—
absolutely <u>FREE!</u>
Please enjoy them with our
compliments...

Jean Gordon

Editor,
Love Inspired Suspense

**Peel off seal and
place inside...**

EDITOR'S
FREE GIFTS
SEAL
THANK YOU

LISUS—EC-11

HOW TO VALIDATE YOUR
EDITOR'S FREE GIFTS!
"THANK YOU"

1   Peel off the FREE GIFTS SEAL from front cover. Place it in the space provided at right. This automatically entitles you to receive two free books and two exciting surprise gifts.

2   Send back this card and you'll get 2 Love Inspired® Suspense books. These books have a combined cover price of $11.00 for the regular-print or $12.50 for the larger-print in the U.S. and $13.00 for the regular-print or $14.50 for the larger-print in Canada, but they are yours to keep absolutely FREE!

3   There's no catch. You're under no obligation to buy anything. We charge nothing—ZERO—for your first shipment. And you don't have to make any minimum number of purchases—not even one!

4   We call this line Love Inspired Suspense because every month you will receive stories of intrigue and romance featuring Christian characters facing challenges to their faith and their lives! You'll like the convenience of getting them delivered to your home well before they are in stores. And you'll love our discount prices, too!

5   We hope that after receiving your free books you'll want to remain a subscriber. But the choice is yours—to continue or cancel, anytime at all! So why not take us up on our invitation, with no risk of any kind. You'll be glad you did!

6   And remember...just for validating your Editor's Free Gifts Offer, we'll send you 2 books and 2 gifts, *ABSOLUTELY FREE!*

YOURS FREE!
We'll send you two fabulous surprise gifts (worth about $10) absolutely FREE, simply for accepting our no-risk offer!

Steeple
Hill ®

The Editor's "Thank You" Free Gifts Include:

- Two inspirational suspense books
- Two exciting surprise gifts

© 2010 STEEPLE HILL BOOKS. PRINTED IN THE U.S.A.

YES!

PLACE
FREE GIFTS
SEAL
HERE

I have placed my Editor's "thank you" Free Gifts seal in the space provided above. Please send me the 2 FREE books and 2 FREE gifts for which I qualify. I understand that I am under no obligation to purchase anything further, as explained on the opposite page.

About how many NEW paperback fiction books have you purchased in the past 3 months?

❏ 0-2   ❏ 3-6   ❏ 7 or more
E9FT   FC4P   FC4Z

❏ I prefer the regular-print edition   ❏ I prefer the larger-print edition
123/323 IDL   110/310 IDL

Please Print

FIRST NAME

LAST NAME

ADDRESS

APT.#   CITY

STATE/PROV.   ZIP/POSTAL CODE

LISUS-EC-11

The Reader Service —Here's How It Works:

any way, I will spend the rest of my life tracking you down. I will stick to you like the Ebola virus, and believe me when I say there will be no treatment that will ease your misery. You got me, Jaden?"

Maddie could not believe what she had heard. Jaden must have, because he nodded solemnly. "Yes, Dr. Ford, I understand."

Paul bent low and headed in the direction from which Jaden reported the snowmobile's approach. Maddie watched until he vanished over the top of the ridge. A terrible numbness took over her body, and she felt as if her legs had turned to lead. Only a tiny bit of warmth remained from the lingering trail of kisses.

"He won't survive," she whispered to no one, feeling the tears gather. "He'll be shot or die in the snow."

Jaden took hold of her shoulder. "You don't know that. Get yourself together and let's move."

She wasn't sure she could. It was as though Paul took her courage with him when he left. Jaden tried a few steps on his own but his ankle gave way and he sank down into snow. The sight of him there, floundering, brought her to her senses.

Giving him her hand, she hauled him up and he hooked an arm around her shoulders. Together they stumbled away from the cabins, toward the thickest section of trees they could find.

It was still dark and the going was rough. She focused on each step—one foot, then another, to put as much distance as they could between themselves and the man on the snowmobile.

Suddenly Jaden stopped, and they squeezed as near a massive fir as they could, until Maddie could feel the rough bark pressing into her side.

"Listen," he mouthed.

The faint rumble of an engine whispered over the snow-banks.

Her heart hammered. "Which direction?"

"Can't be sure. Keep moving."

They went faster now, crunching their way unsteadily through the snow, the ground sloping steeply down. Soon they were panting and sweat-slicked. They paused to listen for the snowmobile engine, but heard nothing. "We'd better stop here. With binoculars, he could spot any movement."

"Do you think he might have gone back? To the crash site?"

"Not until he's sure we're not in the cabins, or Paul's lured him off our path."

Jaden leaned against a tree. His face was haggard, creases cut dark across his forehead. Maddie realized what it was about Jaden's words that seemed out of place.

"You sound like you know all about this guy, the one who's chasing us."

He didn't answer.

"Who is it? How do you know?"

Jaden shook his head. "I don't know anything. And we've got bigger worries right now."

Maddie folded her arms across her chest. "No, I'd say our number-one issue right now is who are you, Tai Jaden?"

She heard the snowmobile engine cough to life.

Jaden stiffened. "Let's go."

"No." Maddie stared straight at him. "Tell me the truth, or I'm not moving."

He grunted. "Then I'll leave without you. I'm not interested in being shot."

She raised an eyebrow. "Fine. Go ahead. See how far you get on that ankle without my help."

He looked at her, his dark eyes glittering, and let out a huge sigh. "Your father was right about you. You're stubborn."

She felt a jolt shoot through her body. "You know my father?"

"Yes, Maddie. I know your father very well. As a matter of fact, I've been working for him for the past few years."

ELEVEN

Paul moved in the direction he figured must be north, toward the side of the mountain where they'd crashed, the feel of Maddie's kiss still tingling through him like sparks of light. The connection he'd always felt to her was just as strong as ever, and he feared the terrible longing would be with him until his last breath. Doubt surged through him in angry waves. Had he done the right thing, leaving her with Jaden? Could she protect herself if he turned out to be after the heart? He wished he had the certainty back, the surety he'd enjoyed in the emergency room. His training, his skills, his natural ability to diagnose quickly and act with precision. Where had all that confidence gone?

There was no time to ruminate. He had to somehow catch the attention of the gunman long enough to draw him away from Maddie and Jaden. He'd heard the engine start up again. Paul pulled out the light stick and made sure the glow was not screened by the trees.

Hey, fella. Here I am. Come and get me.

He stayed out in the open, every so often stepping back behind the trees to scan the horizon for any signs of pursuit, wishing he had a pair of binoculars. The light waned as the chemicals inside wore down.

Desperately, he climbed to a pinnacle of rock and stood there, praying the faint light would be enough.

The snowmobile pulled out from behind one of the tent cabins they'd just abandoned. The driver stopped, engine idling.

He's thinking. Trying to read the situation and the tracks in the snow. Just like the mountain lion sizing up his prey.

If he went in the direction Jaden and Maddie had taken, what would Paul do? There wouldn't be time to reach them before the shooter did. Would they find someplace to hide? The fear clawed at his gut. If he yelled, set off the flare in his emergency pack, the guy might sense it was a distraction and go for the other two.

He forced himself to breathe, fists tight. It was as if he could feel the shooter thinking, reasoning out the most logical way to kill them all.

Paul looked around desperately for something to do, some course of action that might help. His eyes fastened on a wheel-shaped rock nestled precariously in a crack. He crouched down, concealed now behind a snow-covered stump, and pushed and pried at the rock. Though his back was on fire, he forced the rock back and forth until it began to come loose. He kept at it until it gave way, taking with it a cascade of rock and rubble that slid down the precipice, dislodging a river of snow as it did so.

It didn't get far. The loosened debris slid only a few yards before its momentum was checked by the blanket of snow below. Paul was about to look for another stone to loosen when he heard the motor revving.

He stood quickly, making sure the light was visible and the red backpack. Breath burning in his lungs, he watched the snowmobiler head directly for his location. The machine moved over the smooth plane below, idling at the bottom. Paul scanned the area, now beginning to show the faintest traces of gray shadows of dawn.

If Paul climbed, the shooter would have to abandon his snowmobile and climb, too. It was a matter of who could get to a clear spot first, and signal the rescue crew who was hopefully working the crash site on the other side.

The man must have come to the same conclusion, because the motor noise died away and Paul heard from below the sound of feet crunching on rock.

Okay, Ford. Winner takes all in this race.

Above him rose the frozen slopes of the mountain, criss-crossed with gulleys and chasms. It was more a series of separate peaks than a straight vertical climb, and for that he was grateful. The sky was lighter now, the first rays of a brilliant sunrise breaking across the backbone of mountains. He knew that if he could reach a vantage point some hundred feet to his left, he would be able to see the crash site.

As he picked his way along, the cold seeped into his boots. Any warmth he'd felt at being close to a fire, close to Maddie, had disappeared. Why, then, was he sweating, he wondered? Fear? Exertion? He closed his eyes for a moment as the truth dawned.

Infection, probably from the cuts on his back.

The beginning of a fever.

He moved more quickly, leaving the thought behind. There would be no failing this task. Gritting his teeth, he pulled himself up a low ridge of rock. Down below, somewhere off to his right, came the echo of his pursuer. He caught a glimpse of the man between the rocks, moving awkwardly, as if he too had injured himself. Paul couldn't be that lucky.

The man was headed for the same place, the same spot, only rescue was not on his mind. Even if the guy was slightly injured, he was still probably in better condition than Paul.

Paul scanned the snow-covered rocks in desperation. At

this rate, he would be overtaken quickly, before he had a chance to reach his destination. His eyes picked out a twisted trail, a gouge, really, of precarious handholds that led directly to the finish line. Without allowing his mind to focus on the treacherous quality of the path, he began to climb.

The irony took hold, as bits of snow broke away under his feet. Frozen slopes like these had changed the course of his life. When he was fourteen, his mother died in a skiing accident. In the years that followed, his father worked to keep the family afloat, staying eight months at a stretch on an offshore oil rig. Paul assumed it was a dollars-and-cents decision. But as the years passed and he and his brother stayed in the care of Uncle Lyman, Paul realized his father did not want to parent his sons. Whether it was grief over the loss of his wife, or fear at being the parent to two energetic adolescent boys, Paul never knew and never would, since his father died of a heart attack four years after his mother's passing.

He felt a flush of heat in his face and unzipped his jacket a few inches at the top. *Keep climbing, keep moving, get there first.*

The attitude had served him well. It was why he'd decided on medicine. He remembered the moment clearly. At sixteen, he'd taken off deep into the Sierras on a half-baked and ill-prepared backpacking trip. Pockets full of candy, adventure novels and a flashlight. Brilliant.

Night came and found him disoriented, with no idea how to get home and no phone signal to call for help. He'd tried to climb a tree and fallen.

Uncle Lyman found him and took him to a tiny local clinic staffed by one round-cheeked doctor, who was in the process of finishing up Paul's treatment when a pregnant woman dropped to her knees in the lobby.

The doctor sighed, sent Uncle Lyman to the supply closet for materials and turned to Paul. "My nurse is stuck at home because her car won't start. Looks like it's you and me. Are you ready to make a difference?"

A stunned Paul had helped, handing the doctor rubber gloves and instruments, gripping the hand of a woman he did not know until a new life arrived right there on the worn linoleum floor. He'd made a difference and found a passion.

It hadn't always been a smooth journey. Like Mark, he'd tried the alcohol route, too, spending too many nights drinking beer with his uncle and brother, but God had spared him from sharing his brother's fate.

Or *had* he been spared? Could there be any worse agony than watching two children die? He'd never understood why God let those things happen, and truth be told, he was angry God had allowed it to happen to him.

It was not fair or just, as so many other things Paul had encountered in his life.

But God was God, and Paul was not. And the one thing he'd always hung on to was the fact that God saw the entire puzzle, while Paul only caught a glimpse of the pieces.

He remembered his mother. "That's why it's called faith, Pauley. Anyone can believe when things are good. Faith shines brightest in the darkness."

He stopped climbing for a moment and listened. There was no sound of pursuit.

Paul grabbed for another handhold and hoisted himself up, his arms trembling at the effort. The air shook with a rumble, and for a moment he thought he was in the grip of an earthquake. As the noise increased he identified it, heart beating wildly in his chest.

A helicopter.

He could not see it, but the blades cut through the air, vibrating the rocks all around him. Rescue, if he could get to it in time.

Scrambling up as fast as he was able, rocks slid out from

under his feet. The rumble of the helicopter seemed to swallow him up as it grew nearer, until he caught a glimpse of the metal body illuminated by the newly risen sun.

He shouted, though there was no hope of being heard. Pushing forward, urging his beaten body up and up, he moved on.

"Here," he yelled, in spite of himself. "Down here."

He watched in horror as the helicopter moved away and disappeared over the jagged line of the mountain.

His fingers lost their grip and he fell.

Maddie felt the shock shudder through her body. "You work for my father?"

He nodded, listening intently. There was no sound from a snowmobile, so Jaden turned his attention back to her.

"When did he hire you?"

"About a year before the accident."

She gaped. "How come I've never met you?"

He laughed. "There was no need for you to meet me. Most of my tasks were strictly business, many of them overseas. You were busy living your own life, Maddie, and that's the way your father wanted it."

She wanted to grab him by the jacket and shake all the information out of him, but the din of a helicopter drowned out her thoughts. "They found us," she shouted.

Jaden craned his neck upward.

Maddie searched desperately for a glimpse, but did not see it, though the vibrations shook the ground under her feet. After a moment the sound became more distant. "They're leaving," she half sobbed.

He pulled out the radio, but it was still silent, and there was no answer when he spoke into it. He tucked it into his pocket and leaned his back against a tree. "They'll be back. They're doing a quick scan, looking for us."

Maddie could not decide which issue to wrap her mind around first. The helicopter meant that maybe they'd found Paul, gotten to him before the shooter did. Perhaps he was already safe, directing the rescuers back to their location. She should feel overwhelmed with joy at the prospect, but Jaden's revelation echoed in her mind.

"Why didn't you tell me first off you worked for my father?"

"He didn't want you to know. Mr. Lambert wished to keep his business affairs away from the family."

And he had. Maddie wondered for a moment what other business deals her father was involved in that she had no knowledge of. The thought made her uneasy. "So he brought you into this situation because he was worried someone would tamper with the heart?"

"More like concerned that someone might try to make it disappear. That's why I moved it to my possession before we took off. I was following the Heartline driver, and when he stopped to check in at the airport, I took it out of the van. Your father didn't imagine someone would interfere with the flight. If he had, he'd never have allowed you on it."

She remembered the phone conversations they'd had prior to the flight. "He didn't want me to go, anyway." She gazed at the snow as it gradually gained brilliance in the morning sunlight. "Who did he suspect?"

Jaden looked away, up into the sky again. "Rescue team will be here soon."

"Who did my father suspect, Jaden?"

He shrugged. "The hospital in general, the director in particular. He had no love for Dr. Wrigley. The same people you suspect yourself."

"Is that all?"

Jaden finally looked at her. "What are you asking me, Maddie?"

"Did my father think Paul might try to tamper with the Berlin Heart?"

He didn't speak for a moment. "You know the answer to that. Mr. Lambert believes that Dr. Ford let his nieces die. He will pursue a lawsuit to that effect, and that means Dr. Ford has a lot to lose."

"But the plane crash, the shooter. Surely, now he's cleared of suspicion."

"You said it earlier. He might have been double-crossed."

Maddie took a step back, causing her to stumble in the snow and almost fall. "Paul wouldn't do something like that."

"But you accused him and Dr. Wrigley in the caves. You believe the same as your father."

Did she? Her own accusations rang back at her, as strident and bitter as her father's. Did she really believe Paul would be involved in a plot to tamper with the heart? She was cold now, inside the deepest part of her. The facts were clear. Paul had a lot to lose. Her father's death would probably mean the end of the lawsuit. Had the director of the hospital arranged for Paul to take the heart, or damage it in the course of the flight, and then decided to take matters into his own hands?

She knew Paul was ambitious. He'd made no effort to hide the fact that he wanted to be in charge of his own trauma center one day. And he certainly lived for his work. There were many evenings where she shared bad coffee and vending-machine food at the cafeteria, just so she could spend time with him during the busy Saturday night shift.

She felt something else at Jaden's revelation: hurt; only this time, a hurt inflicted by her own father. "Why didn't he trust me to know the truth about you? All this time, and I didn't know the truth."

Jaden sighed. "Maddie, I don't make the rules. I just work

for your father, and he said you were not to know I was in his employ under any circumstances."

"Did he think I would compromise your work because of my past relationship with Paul?"

He shrugged. "As I said, I'm not the decision maker, nor does Mr. Lambert fill me in on his reasoning. I'm paid to protect his interests and follow his orders. That's all."

Her father hadn't trusted her with the truth after all they'd been through. She felt disconnected, dizzy and sick. The strange beeping in her pocket confused her at first, until Jaden hobbled up and grabbed at her hand. "We've got a signal. Your phone is ringing."

With clumsy fingers she grabbed at it. "It's Maddie Lambert. We need help," she gasped.

The connection was filled with static and she moved around, trying to find a better spot. She barely made out her sister's words.

"…all right?"

"We're okay. Katie?"

"Hang on. Rescue teams are—Roger's called. He's on his way here."

She was surprised to hear about Roger, but she had to know the truth. "Katie, how is Dad?"

"…staying…soon."

"What?" She moved again, pressing the phone to her ear and shouting. "Is Dad alive? Tell me, please." There was silence on the other end as the connection died away.

Tears coursed down her face as she flung the phone down in the snow near a pile of rocks.

Jaden spoke softly. "Katie?"

She nodded. "She said Roger is on his way, so at least she's not alone."

"I take it your father doesn't know that."

"My father hates Roger." She didn't know why she said

it. Dirty laundry shouldn't be aired in front of outsiders. But Jaden knew more about her father than she did, it seemed.

Jaden stared at her. "I know."

"Ever since he cheated on Katie. But she never stopped loving him." She swiped at the tears on her face. "I often thought they should have been together when we lost the girls, so he could help her through it, but my father would never permit…" She looked at Jaden through blurry eyes, as a terrible thought struck her. "You don't think it means—" She couldn't finish.

His tone was gentle. "I don't know what it means, Maddie. We just need to get out of here and then we'll know for sure." He pulled out the radio. "I'm going to try again over there, where it's a little higher. I'll be right back."

She tried to take deep breaths, to regain some sense of calm. The panic remained, nestled in her gut. Katie wouldn't allow Roger near their father, for fear of upsetting him in his weakened state. The only reason she could think of why he would be with her was if Maddie was too late, if her father hadn't been able to survive the delayed arrival of the Berlin Heart.

Don't think it. Don't even think it.

Her mind took her back to Paul again, the day she told him about Roger's Huntington's diagnosis. Paul listened in that intense way, holding her hand as he helped her understand the severity of the irreversible disease that would cause Roger's brain to waste away. He talked about dopamine blockers to stabilize the random movements of the body as the nerve cells were compromised, and the promise of a new coenzyme that might help slow the damage. She hadn't heard most of it, but the calm in his voice, the gentle touch of his hand on hers made her believe, whatever happened, he would be there to support Maddie and her sister in any way he could.

Where was Paul now? Had he fallen or been overtaken? She tried to push away the fear.

Feeling the overwhelming urge to move, she crunched forward in the snow toward the massive pile of rocks. Shadowed by the looming mass, she bent low, peering along the ground to find her cell phone, berating herself for throwing it. Katie could call again, and if they could get a signal, then maybe Paul could, too.

She'd heard the phone smack against the rock when she threw it. Trying to reconstruct how far it could have bounced, and hoping she hadn't destroyed it, she looked for any signs that the snow had been disturbed.

The sun was fully risen, and the dazzle of white, mixed with the dark shadow of the rock, made it hard for her to see clearly. Her body stiff with cold, she plodded through the snow, sinking up to her knees in some spots.

She thought again of Paul, the first time he'd gone with her to the snow. A West Coast kid, he'd never really encountered the magnitude of the snow she'd enjoyed on winter trips to Canada with her father and sister. The escapes had become regular after her mother died of cancer, when Maddie was just five. She didn't remember her mother much, but her father had been there always. He'd accepted Paul as Maddie's boyfriend only after much cajoling on her part. Paul had been at his most charming on that one winter trip when he'd joined them.

She remembered him floundering in the snow, constructing a "snow doctor," complete with stethoscope and surgical mask. They'd gone sledding, careening downslope at such an alarming speed, she thought they would wind up in a pile. But Paul relished it. She could see the picture in her mind, his eyes alight, cheeks reddened with cold—and his laugh that always thrilled her—as she clung to his back. They'd crashed all right, directly at the feet of her stern father.

"Just what do you think you're doing?" her father had said.

Paul stood, a clump of snow stuck to the top of his head. "Well, sir, now that I've finished making a mess of sledding, I'm planning on proposing to your daughter, if you have no objections."

There had been none. They both stood openmouthed as Paul dropped to one knee in the snow and produced a little black box with a diamond engagement ring nestled inside.

She'd meant to get rid of that ring, but it still lay in the drawer of her bedroom at her father's house.

Eyes closed, she could still feel his kiss on her mouth, warm and supple, a touch that radiated through her whole body, bringing with it a joy she'd never thought possible. Where had it all gone? All that joy? All that love?

In its place was only anger and blame, and if she was honest, disappointment in the one man she'd thought invincible and perfect. He saved patients on a daily basis, but he did not save Beth and Ginny.

She pictured Mark, safe and warm, getting treatment for his alcoholism. Mark who would live and maybe one day get out of jail to experience all the lovely things in life, which her nieces never would. There was a bitter taste in her mouth.

Pushing the thoughts aside, she renewed her efforts and found the phone nestled in the cold shadow of the boulder. She reached down to get it.

As she straightened, she felt a strange sensation, the feeling of being watched. Her skin prickling in goose bumps, she slowly turned and looked into the golden eyes of the mountain lion crouched on the rock above her.

TWELVE

Paul struggled back to consciousness, finding himself lying between two snow-clad rocks. Waves of heat and cold flashed through his body. He would not have much energy left before the infection took over and left him unresponsive, but he was more worried about another scenario. If the helicopter didn't return soon, Maddie and Jaden might not make it, especially if the shooter had figured out Paul's ruse and went after them.

He pulled himself to his knees, head pounding and eyes blurring, and strained to listen. There was no noise from the climber. Paul tried to figure out how long it had been since the last time he'd heard sounds of the man's progress. With a sickening feeling, he realized it had been quite a while. He'd been so focused on his own climb, on getting to help, he had lost track of his pursuer. He suspected the approach of the rescue helicopter scared the guy.

The man might be on his way back to Maddie and the Berlin Heart. He had to get help, but even pulling himself to his feet required an enormous effort. He was dizzy and becoming unfocused.

Come on, Paul.

He suddenly remembered the flare he'd seen in the pilot's emergency pack. It was now hurriedly crammed in the bottom of his own. With clumsy hands he took out the red cylinder. It was a handheld device. Aiming it away, desperately trying to keep his hands steady, he pulled the cap and fired it into the sky.

It arced upward into the air with a sizzle, streaking over the top of the mountain.

Please God, let them see it.

For good measure, he pulled the crumpled silver emergency blanket out and spread it on the nearest flat rock, hoping it would draw attention from the helicopter he prayed would come. If the shooter was still on the mountain, Paul would be easy prey, but he didn't have the time or energy to fear that possible outcome.

All that mattered was Maddie. He sank down at the foot of the rocks, heedless of the snow that pillowed around him. He was hot, so hot he couldn't stand it. So he unzipped his jacket. Through blurred eyes he watched the sun bathe the ground in radiant sparkles. He was glad. Maddie would be warm. She'd always loved the sun, eating lunch outside, walking the steep San Francisco hills whenever the sunshine beat out the fog.

He saw her now as his hallucination took over, walking up the path, her hair gleaming. She came to him, holding out her hands. From her fingertips hung two pairs of small sandals with tiny flowers stamped in pink, one pink pair, one yellow.

"Maddie," he called, reaching out to her. "Maddie, they're gone. I couldn't save them."

Her expression didn't change. She continued to hold out the shoes to him. "Where are they, Paul? Where are the girls?"

The heat rose in waves through his body, along with a wretched sense of failure. "I couldn't save them. Please believe me. I tried."

Maddie thrust the shoes at him, fingers gripped white. "Why won't you save them? Why?"

He saw angry tears coursing down her face and he knew his was damp, as well. "There was too much damage. I couldn't do it, Mads. Please."

Her face was very pale and he could not find any trace of love there.

"You're a doctor. You have to save them, Paul."

He wanted to turn away, but the powerful condemnation in her voice kept his eyes riveted on her face. "I'm sorry. I'm so sorry."

Finally his mind took pity on him, ending the hallucination by pressing him into unconsciousness.

Paul swam back into reality at the sound of footsteps crunching through the snow. He became aware of three people in orange jumpsuits who seemed to be performing a quick medical assessment on him before they loaded him onto a stretcher and used the helicopter to lift him from his precarious perch on the mountain. As the stretcher rose into the air, twirling, Paul's head began to spin along with it and he lost track of all time. Cold air rushed at him and he wanted to remove his jacket, but he found his arms fastened securely to his sides.

Then they were descending into the waiting hands of a medical team who began to fire questions at him.

"You've got to get Maddie and Jaden."

"Just relax, sir," a medic said and Paul felt the prick of a needle where they started an IV. "Are you Dr. Paul Ford?"

He struggled with his bonds. "Yes. There are three more survivors. Maddie's out there with Jaden. There's a shooter. He wants the heart."

The medic looked at his partner and raised an eyebrow. "We got a call from Maddie Lambert's sister that she is alive. We're canvassing the area now, Dr. Ford. Did the Berlin Heart survive the crash?"

His lips felt as if they were asleep. "Yes. Yes, it survived. You've got to get to Maddie before the shooter does." His head fell back on the stretcher, but not before he heard the medic whisper to his partner.

"Hallucinating."

No. He wanted to shout, to tear loose from the stretcher and haul them along to the place where he'd left Maddie and Jaden. Someone was responsible for the crash, his mind screamed, and whoever it was is after Maddie and Jaden. And Dr. Wrigley. They had to find him, too.

"Help me," was all he could force his mouth to say.

The medic put a reassuring hand on Paul's shoulder. "Just relax, Dr. Ford. We've got people on the way. They'll find the other survivors."

The dark thought coursed through his body as he drifted into unconsciousness. Would they find them in time?

Maddie froze. The mountain lion was crouched low, powerful shoulders coiled and ready to spring. The only thing that moved was a tiny flicker of his nostrils and the silent swish of his tail. Teeth gleamed white and deadly in the cat's mouth. She felt a scream begin to build in her throat. Every atom in her being told her to run, but she remembered Jaden's earlier warning. Don't run. Don't crouch down.

Slowly, inch by painful inch, she straightened, never looking away from those golden eyes. Make yourself big and frightening.

She lifted her arms slowly, trying to ease backward as she did so.

She would be no match for those powerful jaws. One pounce, one bite and she would be dead, her screams muffled by the awful snow. *God.* She felt the words, so long absent, rise in her heart. *God, I need You.*

It could have been a statue, the golden fur gleaming in the sunlight, eyes like cut stones reflecting her fear back at her.

Through her terror, the advice resurfaced in her mind. *Don't run. Make yourself big and threatening.*

She started soft, muted by terror. "Go away, cat."

The animal twitched, ears swiveling.

She said it louder. "Go, cat. Go, go, go." Her voice rose with every syllable until she was shouting it, screaming and waving her arms for all she was worth.

The cat was rigid now, claws digging into the rock, body taut.

She saw the powerful leg muscles tense.

"Please," she whispered, fear choking off the words.

Jaden staggered into view, causing the cat to look away. Maddie used the moment to pull the dead flashlight from her pocket and hurl it as hard as she could at the rock on which the cat was crouched. It smashed into pieces, but the noise startled the cat into action. It turned and leaped away, loping from rock to rock until it disappeared.

She leaned against the tree, hands trembling and breath coming in ragged puffs.

Jaden took her by the arm, his face paler than usual. "I didn't see the lion. I didn't hear a thing until you started yelling."

She managed a nod and felt a flood of tears threaten. Why had she been spared? From the plane crash? From the lion? And why, above all things, had she appealed to God for help? He had allowed her life to fill with unbearable grief.

Her head spun with such violence, she had to lean against a rock to keep from falling. Jaden stood next to her, but she hardly heard him. The last of her strength was gone, and she could only marvel at the fact that her heart was still beating, the blood still pulsing through her body instead of spilled on the snow. She was still alive.

"…called."

Finally, Jaden's words pierced the fog. "What did you say?"

"A rescue team is a half mile from here. I heard via the radio that Katie got through and told them we were alive. They'll be here soon."

He spoke soothingly, softly, as if he were speaking to a child who had taken a fall.

She struggled to her feet, refusing the hand Jaden offered to her. "What about Paul? And my father?"

"They found Paul, but I'm not sure about his condition. I don't have any information about your father."

Every time she thought the nightmare was over, each narrow escape brought with it a new round of horrors, of uncertainty. She felt like a tattered leaf, buffeted by the wind and unable to control her journey, even to the slightest degree. Balling her fingers into fists, she fought the fear and frustration away.

The sound of snowmobile engines rumbled over the snow. Jaden and Maddie both ducked down behind the rocks. Her heart thumped painfully.

In Jaden's wary face, she saw the same question. Were they real rescuers this time? Or was it another chance for the shooter to kill them?

They stayed under cover until the engines stopped and a voice called out. "We're looking for two survivors of a plane crash."

Maddie peeked out from behind the rock and saw two jumpsuited men wearing orange vests and helmets. She stood on shaky legs. Jaden had already limped out of hiding to call to them. One rescuer set about tending to Jaden's ankle while the other approached Maddie.

"Hello. You must be Maddie Lambert."

She nodded, unable to speak for the relief that flooded

through her. This man was for real. He would get her somewhere warm, somewhere safe, and things would be okay.

He moved closer and began questioning her about her
injuries.

She waved him off. "I'm fine. What about Paul? Dr. Ford.
Did you find him? He was on the mountain."

The medic nodded. "We've got him. He's alive."

She would have fallen if he hadn't reached out a hand to
support her. *Joy.* The feeling that bubbled through her could
only be considered joy, but it had been so long since she'd
felt anything like it, she wasn't sure at first. Paul was alive.
He hadn't been shot, or died of exposure or a fall. Paul, the
man who was an integral part of her greatest happiness and
her most horrific tragedy, was alive.

She pictured his gray eyes sparkling with laughter.

"You were worried about me, Mads?" she could hear him
say.

And she had been. Desperately, achingly worried about
him.

Tears started to course down her face, hot and fast and she
could not stop them. Through a curtain of tears, she followed
the medic to a small toboggan attached to the back of the
snowmobile. He eased her into it, strapping her down while
Jaden was secured in the other. The medic took the backpack
from her grip and laid it carefully at her feet.

"My father," Maddie said. "Do you know anything about
my father?"

The medic shook his head. "My job is getting you out of
here."

She wanted to ask him more questions, but he took his
seat on the machine and turned it on.

Then they were bumping over the snow, the impact jar-
ring as they flew along. The exhaust from the snowmobile
engines smelled sour in the pristine air. None of it mattered.

She could think only of her father, of her relief at being taken out of this frozen nowhere.

Of Paul.

She saw Jaden looking around as they traveled, scanning the tree line and the snow, as if he was looking for something.

Not something, she realized.

Someone.

The man who wanted them dead was nowhere to be seen.

Had he given up when he heard the rescue helicopters?

She thought suddenly of Dr. Wrigley. He'd wandered away into the tunnels and she'd been so focused on her own survival she hadn't thought about him. She wondered if he had survived. Or perhaps he had not been able to find a way out. He was an enemy of her father, a man who would celebrate if Bruce Lambert died, but she did not want to think of him lying there in the darkness, waiting for his life to ebb away. She thought about asking the medic about him, but she didn't have the strength to shout over the engine noise.

They skimmed the periphery of the mountain for what seemed an eternity, though it was probably no more than forty minutes. The wind blew cold in her face, freezing her cheeks and making her eyes water. Finally they arrived back where they'd started, the spot where their plane had gone down.

Flames were no longer visible in the wreckage, the whole mass now a blackened mess. The sight of it made her stomach turn. Had it really only been a little more than twenty-four hours since the crash? She did not allow herself to dwell on the memories. As soon as the snowmobile drew up to the center of the rescue operation, she struggled to free herself from the belt.

A helicopter bearing the words Life Flight had set down on a flat section of rock. The rotors were still, but Maddie could see a medic bending over a stretcher inside. It must be Paul. She succeeded in unclipping her belt and freed herself. Grabbing the backpack, she meant to head in his direction, but the medic stopped her.

"We need to get you checked out properly, and we'll fly you to the hospital."

"I want to know about my father. Right now." She tried to keep her voice level, but it wobbled anyway, verging on hysteria.

The medic called over another man, who introduced himself as the leader of the rescue team. "Your father is alive, Ms. Lambert. Very sick, but alive."

It was as if a huge stone had been lifted from her heart. There was still a chance to save her father's life. "We've got to get him this." She held up the pack. "It's a mechanical heart. There's only a few of them in the country. We've got to—"

The man held up his gloved hand. "I've been briefed. There's a helicopter waiting to fly it to your father as we speak. Give it to me and we'll get it to the landing pad."

She gripped the backpack. "Why can't we fly it right now? With that helicopter?"

"We've got patients to transport."

"Patients? Did you find Dr. Wrigley?"

He nodded. "Rescue team found him in the snow. He's not doing well and Dr. Ford is in critical condition."

Her heart squeezed. "Critical? Was he injured?"

He waved off her question. "We need to get them both to the nearest hospital pronto. Let me have the heart. We'll get it to the helicopter and they can get it to your father, check it for damage and get him into surgery."

Still she hesitated, unwilling to let her father's only chance at life out of her sight. Jaden hobbled up and put his hand on her shoulder.

"These guys are legit. They can get it to him faster than we can. Let them take it."

With a swirl of fear that almost swallowed her up, she let go of her precious burden.

THIRTEEN

Paul felt the helicopter lift off and heard the deafening noise of the rotors chopping the air. A hand touched his and he tried to open his eyes but found himself unable to do so. His body burned all over, as if a fire consumed him from the inside.

He was not sure if he was dreaming or awake as he listened to the strange sounds. He heard the pilot radioing to the hospital that they were en route with two critical victims. *Two? Had Maddie been injured? Or worse?*

The helicopter shuddered and pulsed around him and he wondered if the whole thing was a product of fever. Perhaps he was still on the mountainside, lying in the snow, too weak to outrun the shooter any longer.

But someone spoke into his ear, asking him questions, urging him to respond, when all he wanted to do was sink completely into unconsciousness. "My name is Dr. Ford," he heard himself say. Bits and pieces of memory assailed him. Bruce Lambert and the children. A malpractice suit that might strip him of the title of doctor forever. Maddie crying out to him. The feel of her hand on his cheek.

The flight could have lasted for fifteen minutes or hours.

He finally pried his eyes open long enough to look into the

face of a medic in a blue jumpsuit. "We're landing at Greenly Hospital in Olympia, Dr. Ford. Stay awake if you can."

He managed a nod, and then his stretcher was handed out of the aircraft and things began to blur. Rows of fluorescent lights blinked overhead as he was pushed onward. Doors banged open and nurses came and went from his field of vision.

The oxygen mask someone put over his face muffled his voice as he asked them, "Where is Maddie Lambert? What happened to her?"

They patted his shoulder. "You're going to be all right."

He wanted to shout, rip the mask from his face and grab hold of the nearest nurse until he got an answer, but he was too weak to do more than raise a hand. The gesture was ignored.

What followed was a series of examinations, blood draws and an excruciating cleansing of the wounds on his back, which must have rendered him unconscious, because the next thing he knew, he was lying on his side in a hospital bed, an IV hooked up to his arm, listening to the soft beeping of a heart monitor.

At long last a doctor came in, clipboard in hand. She smiled. "Glad to see you awake, Dr. Ford. What a story you must have to tell. Not many people survive a plane crash."

"Or a shooter," he mumbled.

She frowned but didn't answer. "Dr. Ford, I don't have to sugarcoat things for you, since we're in the same profession, after all. You probably want a complete rundown."

He nodded.

"You've got an infection from the lacerations on your back. We're treating you with antibiotics, but so far we haven't broken the fever. You've also got mild frostbite on your toes, but I think we caught it in time. The main thing is, we've got to knock out the infection before it knocks you out." She smiled.

"I want to know about the others. Please."

She closed the clipboard. "Dr. Wrigley is alive but hypothermic. My gut says he'll recover just fine. Mr. Jaden has a badly sprained ankle and dehydration."

Paul held his breath for a moment. "Maddie. Maddie Lambert. How is she?"

"She's fine. Mild frostbite, like you, and a concussion from the crash."

He exhaled so loudly she raised an eyebrow. He didn't care. Maddie was alive. She'd made it through the horrible ordeal.

Thank You, God, he said silently. Another thought raced through his mind and he realized he had no idea how long he'd been lying in the hospital bed. "The Berlin Heart. Can they get it to Bruce Lambert in time?"

The doctor patted his shoulder reassuringly. "It was flown out yesterday. I understand Mr. Lambert had the surgery last evening."

Paul shook his head to be sure he'd heard her correctly. "He's alive?"

She nodded. "He's doing as well as can be expected, I understand."

He sank back and let out a huge sigh. They had actually done it—protected that marvel of biomedical engineering through a plane crash and the snow-covered wilderness, and gotten it to Bruce Lambert in time to save his life. God truly had kept His hand on them the whole time. If he'd had the strength, he would have let out a whoop of joy. At least Maddie still had her father. He pictured her there, standing by his bedside, blue eyes intent on watching for the slightest sign of his coming back to consciousness. Then she would camp out there, sleep on the hard chairs, walk the halls at night to keep herself awake, drink bad coffee and forget to eat.

He felt a stab at his heart and winced.

The doctor raised an eyebrow. "Are you in pain, Dr. Ford?"

He shook his head. "Not the kind you can fix."

She gave him a puzzled look as she left and ushered in a rumpled-looking man, who identified himself as Detective Burton.

Burton shook Paul's hand. "Hey, doc. Looks like you've been through it. Feeling okay?"

"No." Paul suddenly didn't feel like talking about the ordeal for one more moment. He felt nothing but aches, and he suppressed a shudder. "What can I do for you, detective?"

The detective led him through a thorough accounting of the whole affair, which he detailed in his tiny notebook. "So what you're saying is, someone conspired with the copilot to misdirect the plane, maybe to prevent that heart from getting to Bruce Lambert?"

"I suppose so."

"And the folks who would benefit most from that would be…" He made a show of consulting his notebook. "Dr. Wrigley, Stevens, the Director of Bayview Hospital and—" he looked at Paul "—you."

Paul felt the anger burning along with the fever. "If Bruce Lambert dies, it's likely the malpractice suit will, too, that's correct. But I would never be a part of a plot to tamper with a flight, especially one I was a passenger on." The words sounded loud and harsh in the quiet of the hospital room.

"And you wouldn't arrange for someone to shoot at you, now would you, Dr. Ford?"

"No, I wouldn't. That would be ludicrous."

"I agree. Ludicrous. But you wouldn't believe how many

criminal types wind up getting burned by their own fire. Hoisted by their own petard, isn't that the expression?"

Paul didn't like the edge in the man's voice. "Before you say it, I was not part of a plot that went bad, some scheme with the director that took a wrong turn. I don't believe for a moment that the director, or Dr. Wrigley, had anything to do with the crash or the shooting."

"You know," Burton said, taking out a stick of gum and popping it into his mouth, "I wonder if Ms. Lambert will agree with your assessment."

"I'm sure she won't. She's hurt and angry, and she needs someone to blame to get through the loss of her nieces."

"The children Bruce Lambert believes you let die in the E.R.?"

Paul had to take a breath to keep from shouting. If he'd had the strength he would have stood and faced the man. "Yes, that's what he believes."

"And Ms. Lambert? Does she believe it, too?"

He rubbed a hand across his eyes. "You'll have to ask her about that."

"I will," said the detective, riffling the pages of his notebook. "I've spoken with her already, but we need to talk some more."

Paul's anger bubbled over. "Why don't you leave her alone? The woman has been through unbelievable agony. Her father is fighting for his life, and all Maddie wants is to be there and help him recover. She doesn't need you pestering her with questions right now."

The detective looked at Paul for a long moment. When he answered, his voice was cool and hard. "Dr. Ford, I will do whatever I need to do to solve this case. We're looking at two dead pilots and the attempted murder of four other people, not to mention the bringing down of an aircraft. Whoever is involved in any way will be punished to the extent the law will allow, and I will get the information I need to make an arrest any way I deem necessary."

Paul bit back a reply. He'd already antagonized the detective enough for one day.

Burton flipped another page and jotted a note. "One more thing, Dr. Ford. Can you give me a description of the shooter?"

Paul blinked. "No. He wore a ski mask when he first arrived. After that, I never saw his face up close."

"That's too bad. I was hoping you could add some details to our description."

"Description?" Paul sat up so quickly his back rippled with pain. "How did you get a description?"

"Dr. Wrigley saw him up close and personal. The doc found another tunnel to the surface, and emerged at an outcropping of rock. The shooter spotted him, took a few shots, but didn't have a good bead. Wrigley says the guy went off at that point in search of another route, and the doc took that opportunity to escape." Burton walked to the door and turned just before he went out. "So the assassin's got a face now."

Paul struggled upright. "What did he look like?"

The detective shrugged. "Not much to go on, truthfully. Dr. Wrigley was pretty dehydrated…. Tall, dark eyes, old."

"How old?"

"He wasn't sure, but he said the guy was moving real slow and stiff."

"He might be injured. I lobbed a few rocks at him before the cave-in."

Burton looked at him closely. "Does that description ring any bells?"

"Tall and dark-eyed could be anyone. Hard to say."

Burton walked to the door and paused. "We'll continue to talk to Wrigley, and I've got a team checking into the hospital and the director. In the meantime, keep in touch."

Paul read the threat behind the words. "Am I free to leave town?"

"Of course." He smiled, but there was no warmth in it. "Just keep us posted as to your whereabouts."

With a gathering feeling of dread, Paul watched him go.

Maddie snuggled deep under the hospital blanket, even though the room was a comfortable temperature. It was as though the chill of the near tragedy clung to her on the inside. She felt like kissing whoever had invented the blanket warmer. Now that she was safe, emotions raged through her with the intensity of a winter blizzard. Relief at being warm again, out of the elements, rose to the top, along with a hefty burden of guilt.

She should be with her father, at his side when he awoke from his surgery; but instead she was here, being poked and prodded and questioned by the police. The real seed of the guilt lay in the fact that she knew she could have refused admission to the hospital. Though the doctors insisted she should stay, she knew she could have fought their recommendation and walked out the door. Jaden, in fact, had traveled with the heart, refusing to have any medical treatment whatever after his brace was applied. So why was she here instead of en route to her father's bedside? Exhaustion, both physical and emotional, played a part, but she knew the truth lay upstairs, the place where Paul lay, his body ravaged with fever.

As much as she wanted to cut him out of her life, to forget she ever loved him, she could not force her feet to carry her out of the hospital until she knew for a fact he would survive.

What would her father think if he knew she was still tied to Paul so tightly? Why wasn't she strong enough simply to walk away? Her father would have said that Paul let his nieces die, but Maddie could only think of Paul luring the shooter from them, the way he'd threatened to go after Jaden if anything happened to her.

Paul, the bruised and battered man so out of his element, had stayed, determined to save their lives or die trying. Her mind whirled until she pressed her hands to her temples to steady herself.

But you don't love him anymore, Maddie. He'll forever be tied to the worst moment in your life.

She could no longer bear lying there. In spite of a wave of dizziness, she forced herself upright and was attempting to stand, when the phone next to her bed rang. She collapsed back on the bed and answered.

"Maddie?"

"Yes."

Her sister's voice filled the line, and there were tears and incoherent sobbing on both ends. Maddie couldn't speak for a moment, so she let her sister do the talking.

"Oh, Maddie. I thought you were dead. I can't believe you survived a plane crash and some crazy lunatic. The police said they haven't caught the shooter, but they have a description from Dr. Wrigley. Are you okay? Is everyone else okay?"

Wrigley had seen the shooter? It figured that the only person who had actually seen the shooter was a man she didn't trust a whit. "The pilots didn't survive, but the rest of us are okay for the moment. Wrigley is going to be released soon, the nurse told me. I have a concussion, but I'll be fine, too."

Katie let out a gust of air. "I couldn't believe it when the authorities told me what happened. I tried your cell phone a million times, and when there was no answer…I almost went crazy. Then Roger called after he heard about the crash. I think I would have lost it if he didn't talk me down. He should be here any minute." She lowered her voice. "Don't worry,

Maddie, Dad doesn't know he's coming. We don't want him upset."

She could hear the unspoken plea in her sister's words. "Katie, I'm glad Roger is going to be there with you. I'm so happy you weren't alone through all this."

"Me, too." Katie sobbed quietly into the phone.

Maddie gave her sister a moment to compose herself before she asked, "How is Dad?"

Katie let out a sigh. "He's okay. The doctors say he's responding in all the ways they'd hope for after a transplant."

Maddie blinked back the tears. "You don't know how happy I am to hear that."

"It's because of you he's still with us. You delivered the Berlin Heart in one piece."

"I had help. Paul kept us alive, really, and Tai Jaden."

Her sister's voice grew hard. "Paul? Paul Ford? You are kidding me, Maddie. How could you let that man help you with anything?"

She gripped the phone. "We were alone in the wilderness, Katie. He is the reason I'm alive. I can't lie about that."

There was a pause. "Well, I guess I will thank him for that, but I'll never forgive him, Maddie. Never."

Maddie exhaled. "I'll come the first chance I get."

"Okay. My other line is ringing. I think it's Roger."

She hesitated, remembering how this man had hurt her sister. "Thank him for me, Katie."

She disconnected and allowed herself to think about the irony of the situation. Roger, the man who cheated on his wife, was now a source of comfort and support; but Katie would never forgive Paul, nor did she want Maddie to.

A snippet of *Proverbs* tickled her memory from some long-forgotten Sunday school class. "Do not let kindness and truth leave you."

But they had. The moment her nieces died, she felt all the sweetness of her soul dry up and blow away in a cloud of bitter pain. Had the truth gone with it, too? She'd thought the truth was clear. Paul enabled his brother to drive drunk, and what was worse, he gave up on saving her nieces to tend to his injured sibling.

It was the truth, plain and simple. Paul would pay by losing his license. Her father would see to it.

So why did the truth sit so painfully in her gut now? She pictured Paul there in the snow, bruised and bleeding, pulling her from the ice tunnel, leading the shooter away.

Why had he done it?

Guilt? The need to make up for his failure in the emergency room?

She had to get out of the hospital and to her father, but first she needed to find Paul and set things straight in her own mind.

She sat up more slowly this time, allowing the spinning in her head to subside before she planted her feet on the floor and reached for a smock lying on a chair. She pulled it around herself like a robe. The tile under her feet was cold, even through the thick socks the hospital had provided. The sense of disbelief crowded her mind again. Was she really here, safe and sound inside these sturdy walls?

She passed by many doors, some with sleeping patients inside, others empty, waiting for the next occupant to come along. The door on the end stood open and she heard a familiar voice.

"No. I barely survived. I think I've done my duty."

It was Wrigley's voice, she was sure. Her heart beat a quick staccato. Was he talking to the director? Would he say enough to incriminate himself in the plot to keep her father from getting the life-saving surgery?

She edged closer, hoping no hospital employees would

make an appearance. Peeking around the door, she saw Dr. Wrigley propped up against the pillows, one hand gripping his cell phone. His face was pale and drawn, harsh lines bracketed his mouth. He was so intent on his conversation he didn't notice her standing there.

"Whatever Lambert does is his business. Nearly being gunned down on a mountainside has changed my perspective. I'm getting out of here today and I'm going home. I'll be content never to leave California again."

Wrigley shook his head. "Our deal is off. However you want to handle things from here on is your business." He slammed down the phone and looked up, eyes widening as he saw her. "Ms. Lambert, I—I didn't realize you were there."

She strode into the room. "I'll bet. Who were you talking to?"

He gave her a weak smile. "Director Stevens. He was just checking in on me."

Maddie folded her arms. "I don't think so. I heard the whole thing. What were you doing for the director?"

"Nothing, nothing at all."

She came closer to his bed. "All of this is going straight to the cops, Dr. Wrigley. I'll tell them everything I heard, and it will be quite a while before you get back to California."

His shoulders slumped. He plucked at the edge of the blanket until he seemed to come to a decision. "All right. I'll tell you everything, and you can do with it what you want to. At this point, I have no loyalties to anyone but myself. I'm resigning my post, anyway." He paused. "Director Stevens was worried that your father would find some, er, irregularities in the books."

"He'd been stealing from the hospital?"

"No, not stealing, just moving money around to make the financial picture a bit rosier for the stockholders."

"And you helped him?"

"Not at first. I didn't even know about it until he came to me when your father started his investigation. He pointed out how it was in my best interest to see the investigation go away."

"Why?"

"Because if the hospital was bought out, the new owners would bring in their own staff of people, and I'd likely lose my position as head of the E.R."

"So what did you do?"

Wrigley looked at a spot on the ceiling.

"Dr. Wrigley, what did you do?"

FOURTEEN

At first she thought he was not going to answer. The silence crept on until Dr. Wrigley sighed.

"I arranged for your father's car to be broken into and his laptop stolen. It wouldn't be enough to stop the investigation, but the director wanted your father distracted until he could cover up some of his bad decisions."

"So that was you?" Maddie shook her head in disgust. "And were you supposed to tamper with the heart? Was that another of your assignments from the director?"

"No." He stared straight into her eyes. "Whatever you think of me, I'm a doctor—and I would never cause harm intentionally."

She huffed. "You don't consider theft and vandalism harmful?"

Wrigley ignored her comment. "The director wanted me to accompany the heart and make a show of goodwill. He was hoping your father would think more kindly of the hospital, since we moved mountains to arrange for the acquisition of the heart. The director thought that maybe your father could even be persuaded to drop the malpractice suit and walk away from his investigation."

Maddie thought about her father, the man who had never walked away from any kind of fight. How little they knew him. Wrigley's expression told her he knew the truth, as well.

"I told him Lambert would never give up, but he didn't listen."

She looked at Wrigley, trying to read the sincerity on his face. "Dr. Wrigley, do you think the director arranged to have the copilot take us off course? Is that why you're resigning your post?"

He exhaled, and his face appeared far older than it had when she'd first seen him on the plane. "I'm walking away because I don't recognize myself in the mirror, Ms. Lambert. I got into medicine to save people, and lately all I've been thinking about is saving myself." His lower lip quivered. "Now, if you'll excuse me, I'm going to rest. I'm pushing to be discharged shortly."

Maddie turned and left the room. She had no idea if Wrigley was to be believed. Was he privy to more than he was admitting? The defeat in his face seemed real enough, but she did not trust her own judgment anymore. Her father would never fall for lies. He would have dismissed Wrigley's story outright.

She took the elevator up to the ICU and asked the nurse about Paul.

She pointed. "Down the hall, room nine."

Maddie found the room. Her heart beat faster with each step she took. Part of her wanted to run the other way, to avoid facing the man who caused her emotions to tangle up like a tumbled skein of yarn. In spite of her reluctance, she found herself crossing the threshold.

Paul was asleep. His face was shadowed with bruises, but she thought she could detect some color in his cheeks. He looked vulnerable lying there, so unlike the confident man who strode around the emergency room directing things like the conductor of an orchestra.

She sat at the chair by his bed. Who was he really? The tender person who loved her in ways she never dreamed possible? A person blinded by love of his brother, who turned his back on two small children?

Maybe more to the point was, who was Maddie Lambert? A woman who trusted and loved her fiancé? Or an embittered soul who wanted nothing but revenge, like her father? She didn't know anymore. The path of her life, which had seemed so certain before, so straight and clear, was mired in confusion. Where was the truth in all the mess?

She saw his eyes open sleepily, and widen as they locked on hers.

He reached out a hand and she took it. "How are you feeling?"

"Better." He squeezed her fingers. "Docs say the fever is coming down. Antibiotics are doing the job."

She tried to keep the heady rush of relief from her voice. "That's so good to hear."

He kept hold of her hand. "You look good. Are you supposed to be wandering around the hospital?"

She pulled away. "It's a good thing I have been." She related to him what Wrigley had told her.

"I never thought the director or Wrigley would be involved in something like that, but it doesn't explain who drugged the pilot and shot at us."

"No, it doesn't prove anything, unless Director Stevens paid off the copilot. Or Wrigley knows more than he's telling. Jaden doesn't trust them."

"Jaden?"

She watched Paul's surprise as she told him about Jaden's connection to her father. "Jaden said my father hired him because he didn't trust anyone from Bayview." She shifted uncomfortably, pulling away from him and fiddling with the water cup on his bedside tray. "I guess he didn't trust me to know about Jaden, either, for different reasons."

He looked closely at her. "What are you thinking about?"

She took a deep breath. "I wanted to apologize for implying you had something to do with trying to sabotage my father's heart. I was upset, but it wasn't fair to blame you."

He was quiet, so quiet she found herself unsure how to proceed.

He sighed. "Thanks for saying that. I know I'll never convince your father—" he shook his head "—or you that I'd never hurt your family on purpose. Every day I think about my decision to trust my brother, and every day I convict myself for that choice. More than anything, I regret that I could not comfort you when you needed me most. To watch you hurt is even worse than the pain I carry around. Do you believe that, Mads?"

"Yes," she heard herself whisper. She wanted to curl up next to him and kiss the worry lines from his forehead. She started forward and stopped abruptly. Things hadn't changed. They were still stuck at the same crossroads of grief and blame as they had been before. Her father would recover, and he would set out to ruin Paul and the hospital. And he would expect her to help him do it.

Maddie backed toward the door. "I'd better go."

"When are you being released?"

"Tomorrow." Though she didn't look at him, she felt his gaze on her face.

"Will you fly to your father's place?"

A shudder coursed through her. "I'll find someone to drive me. I don't think I want to board a plane again for a while."

He nodded. "I understand."

"What about you? What will you do?"

He looked at her with such sadness she felt her heart lock up with grief.

"I'm not sure." He gave her a wan smile. "Odd to hear me say that, isn't it?"

She didn't tell him how it broke her heart to see him so uncertain. "Goodbye, Paul."

It took all Paul's powers of persuasion the next day to convince the doctor he should be released. If the situation was reversed, he wouldn't have discharged himself either, but the fever had broken. He was weak and fatigued, but after Maddie's visit, he knew it was the only choice possible. He had to go and help her.

The doctor finally relented and handed him a bag of antibiotics and the number for a car-rental place, which promised to have a vehicle waiting in the hospital parking lot. Paul confirmed his plan as he pulled on the clothes he'd been wearing when rescuers plucked him off the mountain. Maddie should not drive herself to the hospital where her father was recovering. It was a good four-hour trip, and she'd sustained a concussion. He would take her before he returned to San Francisco. It was purely a practical decision.

Deep down, he knew it had nothing to do with the practical. He wanted to be close to her, even for a few more hours, to savor the intimacy that he understood would disappear as soon as she got back to her father. After that, he would have to learn to live without her permanently, seeing her only in court perhaps, when her father came after him with both barrels. His back stung as he put on the shirt and bent to tie his shoes.

The physical danger to Maddie and himself was past. The shooter, who may or may not have been hired by Director Stevens, had no reason to come after them anymore. Bruce Lambert had received the heart and the police were looking at the director under a microscope. There would be no more attacks, he felt certain. Jaden was there to look after Maddie and her father. All the same, he felt a tinge of worry down in his gut.

Probably post-traumatic stress, he told himself. Nonetheless he hurried as much as he was able, to get to Maddie's room before she was released.

He made it a moment before she was ready to leave. She started when she saw him. "What are you doing here?"

"Driving you. I rented a car."

She shook her head—a little gingerly, he thought.

"No. Absolutely not. You should stay here. I can call for a car."

"Already done." He gestured toward the door. "Shall we?"

She stared at him, shaking her head. "I don't want you to drive me."

"Why not? I'm a great driver. Only four parking tickets last year, and that last one was certainly not my fault."

She opened her mouth but didn't answer. They both knew exactly why she refused. Too much pain, too much anger. He didn't give her time to voice the thoughts as he wrapped an arm around her shoulders and moved her to the door.

"Paul, this isn't a good idea."

"Come on, Mads. I've filled my pockets with candy from the vending machine. Four hours of sparkling conversation and sugar. Then we're done." He felt her stiffen under his grasp.

"Then you'll leave?"

He forced a smile. "Of course. That's what you want, isn't it?"

The unanswered question hung heavy in the air as they headed for the elevator.

* * *

In a few minutes, they were packed into the rental car and heading to the freeway. Traffic was light as they traveled north. Maddie remained quiet the first hour of the journey, staring out the window. He remembered their day trips prior to the accident, how he'd loved to listen to her talk about anything and everything. It was as if the tragedy had stripped away their past, covered over the good times until they seemed like someone else's memories.

He finally couldn't stand the silence any longer. "How are you feeling?"

She didn't look at him. "Stiff and banged up, but otherwise fine." She played with the zipper on her jacket and shot him a sideways glance. "What about you? You look pale. I don't think they should have discharged you."

"I'm peachy." In fact, Paul was fighting a headache and weariness that seemed to have settled deep in his bones. He tried to catch her eye, but she had already turned toward the window again. What had he hoped to accomplish by driving her? Maybe it would have been better for them both if he left directly from the hospital, and they'd gone their separate ways. He should go home and check in on Mark.

What was the use? His brother would be living the imposed sobriety of prison life, but would he ever have the strength to kick the addiction on the outside? And would he ever have the chance to try? Did he even want to?

Paul sighed and Maddie started.

"What are you thinking about?"

He didn't have the energy to come up with a witty reply. "My brother."

She was silent for a moment. "What in particular?"

The truth came out before he had a chance to think better of it. "I'm afraid that he's lost, so badly lost that I can't save him. I've tried, I've done everything. And even though I'm a doctor and I've saved more lives than I can count, I couldn't save him."

Her tone was bitter. "But he's alive, Paul. You did save him."

"His body is alive, but he is so torn up about the accident, I can't even see the man who used to be my brother."

She shifted. "Even though things turned out the way they did, no one could say you didn't try everything to help him."

"It wasn't enough. I couldn't find the treatment, the prescription, the one thing that would help him kick the addiction. I don't know what I did wrong." He felt a thickening in his throat and he coughed to cover it, surprised when Maddie put her hand on his knee.

"It wasn't your battle to win, Paul."

He must be imagining the tender tone in her words. The road seemed to darken ahead of him. "I failed. I failed everyone."

"You did what you could."

The irony was too much. "Not in the eyes of your father, or yours."

He heard her take a deep breath, her fingers tightening on his knee, but he kept his gaze directed forward.

"Paul, when we were together, when things were good before…" She paused for a moment. "You told me that the saving part, the life-or-death part, was God's job, He just let you hold the scalpel."

"I guess I did."

"Do you still believe that?"

The question convicted him. It rang like a bell through his heart. "I don't know." His own arrogance, the unswerving belief in his own abilities, left a bitter taste.

"Your brother may or may not be saved, but maybe it isn't in your power, one way or the other."

He was afraid to utter the thought, scared to sever the connection between them, the fragile thread that bound them together at that moment. "You're right. I got cocky, began to think my skill as a doctor allowed me to decide things. I've been arrogant and prideful." He turned to her. "But, Mads, you know I did everything I could think of to save Mark." He forced out the words. "Just like I did everything for Beth and Ginny. You believe me, don't you?"

She looked at him, eyes glistening with moisture, mouth open to speak.

He knew that his future, his only remaining chance at happiness, lay in the words she was about to utter. Abruptly, she pulled her hand away and sat back in the seat, eyes closed, lips tight.

There's your answer, Paul. She will never believe you. Ignoring the scorch of pain in his heart, he refocused on the road.

Her phone rang and she answered it. "It's Jaden. He's at the hospital with my father." She listened for a moment and he heard her delighted gasp. "Jaden says my father got the breathing tube out. He's floored the doctors with his progress."

"I'm not surprised at all. If anyone could prove a doctor wrong, it would be your father."

He looked at her profile, face shining with excitement, mouth parted in that smile that always made him weak in the knees. The pain in his heart worsened and he fought it down. He would not be a part of her joy, or her life, once they reached their destination. He would have to learn to live without her.

Suddenly Maddie's tone changed. "Why? It's all over, isn't it? The police are investigating Director Stevens and Dr. Wrigley. They wouldn't dare try anything else."

Paul saw the fear trickle over her face again.

She gripped his fingers and clenched the phone to her ear.

"I'm driving with Paul. We'll be there in a couple of hours. Are Katie and Roger with you?"

Maddie finished the conversation and closed the phone. "He doesn't think the threat to my father is gone yet."

Paul didn't answer, but he agreed with Jaden. He had no particular reason for his position, other than a nagging feeling in his gut that something wasn't quite right.

"How is your sister?"

"Roger got there and insisted she go back to my father's house for a rest this morning, but she refused. At least I know she's being taken care of." Maddie shook her head. "The first thing my father said when they removed the tube was he wanted to go home."

Paul laughed. "Why am I not surprised?"

She turned troubled blue eyes in his direction. "Paul, what if Jaden's right? What if there is still some sort of plot afoot to kill my father?"

"From some other enemy we don't know about?"

She shrugged. "I don't know."

He tried to think it through. "Your father has passed the critical point. Now he's just got to recover and regain his strength. Jaden will stay at his side, along with you and your sister. He'll have people keeping a watchful eye over him."

She began to play with her jacket zipper again. "I suppose so."

He thought about offering to stay nearby until Bruce Lambert was back to full speed. He grimaced. At least then Bruce wouldn't have to work too hard to find Paul when he was ready to bury him for good. But Maddie had made it clear that they could not ever cross the strained distance that separated them.

They both retreated into silence as the miles passed by. She refused his offer of chocolate, so he devoured the candy bar mechanically, not really tasting the flavor. With an hour to go, Paul stopped at a diner, insisting that they at least get coffee and sandwiches. His back was sore and he worried that, without a jolt of caffeine, he might not be able to complete the last hour of the drive. The sun was low in the sky and the temperature was dropping rapidly as they climbed out of the car, both of them stiff.

Maddie cracked a smile. "We look like a couple of old folks."

He smiled back. "I think, after all we've been through, we might have aged a couple of decades." He led her inside and they settled into an orange, upholstered booth, ordering grilled cheese sandwiches and coffee.

A TV fixed above the counter blared the latest news.

Paul wished his mind would catch up with the situation. Days ago, they'd been on a crashing plane, and now here they were, sipping coffee at a diner. He saw, from the slightly bewildered look on Maddie's face, that she was struggling to adjust, as well.

Maddie stared at the TV, a coffee cup held between her hands. He was about to try and make conversation when she bolted upright, coffee cup crashing to the floor at her feet.

"Paul," she said, her voice the barest whisper. "Look," she said, pointing a trembling finger at the television screen.

FIFTEEN

Maddie stared at the television in horror. A photo of Dr. Wrigley was displayed as the reporter read the story.

"This morning a car was pulled from an aqueduct by local firefighters. Inside the vehicle was the body of a man later identified as Dr. Matthew Wrigley, lead surgeon at Bayview Hospital. According to police, Wrigley died of a gunshot wound to the head. Ironically, the victim had recently survived a plane crash and was on his way back to his San Francisco home after his discharge from an area hospital. The investigation into Dr. Wrigley's murder is ongoing."

The reporter smoothed some papers in front of her and moved on to introducing the weather.

Maddie was vaguely aware of Paul pulling her over to his side of the booth. His arm was around her shoulders, apologizing to the waitress that arrived to clean up the spilled coffee. When she left, he spoke quietly.

"It's going to be okay. Breathe slowly through your nose."

She tried to comply, but her breath came in gasps. "He's dead. He's been shot."

Paul squeezed her close and she put her head on his shoulder, rubbing her cheek against the hard muscle. The feel of him there, his arm around her, was all that kept her from losing it completely. Her nerves were on fire, panic shooting through them like blasts of electricity.

"We don't know the details, Mads. It could be unrelated."

"No," she whispered. "I'm sure it was the same person who tried to kill us in the mountains."

He stroked her arm. "Let's not jump to conclusions."

She wanted to scream as she jerked away and stared into his face. "You don't believe it's a coincidence, that this was some random drive-by shooting."

He slowly shook his head. "No, I don't."

"What should we do?"

"I think we should call the police and find out what they know and how we can help."

The blood still rushed in her ears. "Yes, you're right." The need rose in her, intense and terrible. "We can call from the car. I've got to get to my father."

Paul said something but she didn't hear, she was already halfway to the door. She slammed out into the cold air, thick, dark clouds starting to empty frigid sleet down upon them.

He joined her in a few moments, handing her a hastily wrapped sandwich before they got in. "At least eat something while we drive."

She couldn't force down a bite. Teeth chattering, she dialed the number of the local police. They patched her through to Burton, the detective who had taken her statement in the hospital.

"We can't discuss the details right now, Ms. Lambert. We've got officers looking into it and forensics is running an analysis."

"Someone wants my father dead. He needs protection."

Burton sighed. "We've got an officer posted at the hospital as a precaution, but he tells me your father is insisting on being sent home to recuperate. He's gone so far as to hire private nurses and have a hospital bed delivered to his home."

She groaned. Her father's attitude didn't surprise her, and she couldn't entirely blame him after what happened with his nieces. "Can you provide protection for him at home?"

"We're not in the business of loaning out cops, but we'll certainly arrange for someone to check on him regularly, until the investigation is closed."

She all but shrieked, "Someone wants my father dead."

"We're looking into the situation, Ms. Lambert. It could be Wrigley's murder has nothing to do with your father."

"I don't believe that."

"Frankly, I don't either, but your father has made plenty of enemies."

She snuck a glance at Paul. Yes, her father had many enemies and the man sitting next to her in the car could be counted among them. She wondered what her father would say if he knew how Paul had helped her, held her together through the ordeals she'd faced. Would it change his mind in any way?

Picturing her father's determined face, she didn't think so. The detective promised to keep her informed. She made sure he had her cell number and the number at her father's house before she hung up. "How much longer?"

Paul looked at his watch. "About twenty minutes."

Gritting her teeth, she silently urged the car to go faster, but traffic in the city and the icy roads slowed them down. It was evening when they reached the hospital. Paul dropped her at the entrance.

"I'll go park the car and meet you."

Maddie felt a surge of relief. She knew he intended to leave as soon as he delivered her, but she was grateful he would stay awhile longer.

He's just comfortable, a familiar face in the middle of the storm. As soon as things were a bit more settled, he would leave and they would return to their separate worlds, strangers to one another. The realization sparked an ache in her which she pushed away while she hastened across the slick sidewalk.

The nurse at the admitting desk told her where to find her father and she headed up immediately, pleased that he was no longer in the ICU. She passed a waiting area and did a double take.

Roger was there, his arm around Katie. They both looked up at the same time and broke into enormous smiles.

Katie wrapped her arms around Maddie and they cried together.

"It's a miracle," Katie said, hiccuping. "A God-given miracle that you're still alive."

It *was* a miracle, Maddie thought suddenly. She'd been given a miracle when she hadn't even had the strength to ask for one. The idea took her completely by surprise. She kissed her sister and Roger wrapped her in a hug. The five years since she'd seen him had left their mark on his face. His dark hair was streaked with gray and shadows rimmed his eyes.

He smiled at her. "You made good time."

"How's Dad?"

Katie wiped her eyes. "He's doing brilliantly, but the doctors still want him to stay here while he recovers. Of course, he's having none of it."

Maddie sighed. "I was told he's checking himself out."

"Tomorrow," Roger said. "We stalled him that long, anyway."

We? Roger must have seen the question on Maddie's face.

"He doesn't know I'm here with Katie, and we'll keep it

that way until he's got his strength back. Then he can go at me full speed."

They all laughed. Maddie wanted to ask if he and Katie planned to try to repair their broken relationship, but she didn't think it was the time to ask. "Did you hear about Dr. Wrigley?"

Roger nodded. "They called here a few hours ago and a police officer showed up to camp outside your father's room. I heard Wrigley saw the shooter. Do you think that's why he was killed?"

Maddie shrugged. "It makes sense."

Roger lowered his voice. "And you think this same person is really after your dad?"

Maddie nodded. "I'm certain of it."

Roger sighed. "Mr. Lambert is ruthless, but I can't believe someone would go to so much trouble to kill him."

"I think the person who shot at us is the same one who killed Wrigley."

Roger shook his head. "I heard the pilot might have been drugged."

Katie paled. "But how could whoever drugged him know where you'd crash?"

"Jaden thinks the copilot was going to meet someone. If that's true, the shooter was already in the general area," Maddie said.

Roger looked grim. "And he could have connections to someone in air-traffic control. Paid an employee off to alert him when the emergency locator transmitter went off."

Maddie nodded. Roger used to manage the accounts for a private fleet of jets, so she trusted his theory. "He was probably hoping none of us survived." She shivered. "We almost didn't."

Katie's eyes widened and she put a trembling hand to her mouth. "I wanted to believe this nightmare was over."

The elevator doors opened and Paul stepped out.

Katie blanched. "But I see it's just beginning."

Paul hesitated when he saw Katie. The horrified look on her face quickly morphed into an expression of hatred. She stepped forward.

"What are you doing here?" she seethed.

Maddie put a hand on her sister's shoulder. "He brought me. I can't drive with a concussion."

Katie stared at him. "Okay. You drove her. Thanks for that. Now you can go."

Maddie stepped between them. "He doesn't have to leave."

Katie started as if she'd been slapped. "I don't want him here. I don't understand why you would want to be anywhere near him, Maddie."

Maddie's voice softened. "He kept me alive, Sis. I wouldn't be standing here if it weren't for him."

Tears filled Katie's eyes. "But he didn't keep my babies alive, my sweet girls." She wrapped her arms around herself and looked at the floor. "Tell me how I'm supposed to handle that, Maddie. Should I be happy to see him after his brother killed my children?"

Paul ignored the pain burning inside his gut. He'd made a mistake coming here. "I think I'm making things more difficult for you all. I'd better leave." He'd made it a few steps away, but Maddie grabbed his wrist. Her fingers were so soft against his.

"Whatever happened in the past, my sister needs to know that you saved my life."

He looked into her blue eyes, unable to speak as she led him back to the waiting area.

"Katie," she said, "I want Paul to stay until we get Dad settled. He's still recovering from the crash and it's not safe for him to leave tonight."

Katie looked from Paul to her sister. "Do you think Dad would want him here?"

Maddie lifted her chin and Paul saw the gleam of determination in her face that he hadn't seen for a long while. "Dad wouldn't want Roger here either, but the fact is, you and I need help to get through this."

Katie bit her lip and Roger moved next to her. "Your sister is right, Katie. We've got to do whatever we need to, until your father is out of danger."

Maddie shot him a grateful look.

Paul watched, still uncertain whether or not he should be there. He did not want to be looking into the anguished faces of parents whose children he hadn't been able to save, but more than that, he did not want to walk away from Maddie when she needed him.

Roger continued. "I think I should take Katie home for a while. She's been here since sunup, and she's only eaten half a sandwich. Besides, we'd better get things set up for your dad's hospital bed, because he's going to bully his way out of here one way or the other."

Maddie nodded. "You know him too well."

Roger raised an eyebrow. "I sure do. Will you be okay here for a while?"

Maddie nodded. "Yes, I want to spend time with Dad. You two go home and I'll see you in the morning."

Katie embraced her again and avoided looking at Paul as they made their way to the elevator.

"I—I hope that was okay, to tell them you were staying." He saw a flush of pink on Maddie's cheeks.

"I'm here as long as you need me."

Her fingers found the jacket zipper. "You need some rest. I can ask if there's a room where you can lie down."

"Nah. There's a chair in the waiting area with my name on it." He felt as if he stood on shifting ground. She'd asked him to stay. Probably, she was afraid he'd collapse on the road somewhere. He wouldn't give her any more reason to worry.

She suddenly came to him, folding him in a gentle embrace. He rested his chin on her head as he had a million times before, and let her fragrance fill up his senses. She turned her face to his neck and he felt her lips there, grazing his throat. Paul allowed himself to pretend for a blissful moment that things were the way they used to be and there was only love between them.

Then she pulled away and his heart went with her.

A gleam of moisture shone in her eyes. "I wanted to say I'm sorry for bringing you here to face things. My sister is so angry, and she can't forget what happened."

The words felt as if they were torn from his mouth. "Can *you?*" He wanted to hold her again, to bring back the closeness that still sang through his nerves.

She shook her head. "It's not the time to figure it out. I'm still angry that God let it happen. Why couldn't it have been another doctor on duty that night?"

"I've asked that same question again and again. And you know what I think the answer is?"

"What?"

"Because no one would have worked harder to save those little girls than I did. The real question is, why didn't He let me succeed?"

Her voice trembled. "Do you think you'll ever know why, Paul?"

"No, Mads. Not until I come face-to-face and ask Him. As much as it tears me apart, some things are only God's to know."

She took a step back, face hardening. "It's not fair."

"I agree."

"So that's how you sleep at night? Believing you did your

best, and it was God's will to take those girls?" Her tone was bitter, but there was earnestness underneath, a vulnerable little girl peeking out with longing.

"That's what I believe, Mads." He sighed, feeling bone-tired. "But I still don't sleep at night."

She looked at him a moment longer, then turned and went past the police officer into her father's room.

He trudged to the nearest chair in the gloomy waiting area. The room was cold, but he still felt residual warmth from their embrace. The sensation stayed with him as he looked around at the dog-eared magazines and the bedraggled potted plant in the corner. The irony hit him full force. He'd spent most of his adult life in hospitals, going from patient to patient, sometimes meeting families in chairs exactly like these, delivering news that would devastate them. Each time he'd prayed beforehand.

Lord, help me deliver the truth gently.

Now his prayer was different.

Lord, help Maddie find her way back to You.

When he left, she would have only a vengeful father and a sister broken by grief. She would need His grace to bring her back to the joyful soul she had been before the accident.

Paul jerked awake two hours later, groaning from a kink in his neck. Another cop was stationed outside the door now, looking supremely bored.

Paul tried to get back to sleep, but the waiting-room chairs were hard and not a good fit for his tall frame.

In order to work out some of the stiffness in his back, he strolled the hallways until he found a sort of atrium, with groups of chairs and tall plants that reached up toward the skylight. There were a few doctors there, deep in conversation. He was about to return to see if Maddie needed anything, when his attention was caught by the sight of two familiar men in the corner. Tai Jaden and Roger stood talking, unaware of his presence.

Something about their body language told him it was not an idle chat. Jaden had lied to them and Paul had an unrelenting feeling the man was not to be trusted. He knew Maddie did not see it the same way, and she was far too concerned about her father to spend time looking closely at motives. He felt it was his duty to keep apprised of the situation for her.

Paul eased closer, staying behind the border of plants.

Roger laughed, but the sound held no humor. "Why should I care? You are an employee of Bruce Lambert, nothing more. You're not family, and you don't have a vested interest in seeing him recover, except to protect your paycheck."

Paul didn't catch Jaden's response, so he eased closer. He saw Roger's face pinched in a scowl. "If you really want to help out, why don't you catch this nutcase who is out shooting at people?" Roger's eyes narrowed. "Or maybe you have some reason why you don't want him caught?

Jaden had his back to Paul, but Paul saw him tense.

"I'm following some leads on that," he heard Jaden say.

"I'll bet." Roger shook his head. "Look, I just came back to arrange for delivery of the hospital bed. I don't like leaving Katie in that big house alone. I've got to go."

Jaden made another comment which Paul couldn't make out as Roger left, knocking into a plant as he departed.

Paul walked over to Jaden, who seemed to be lost in thought. "Hello, Mr. Jaden. How's the ankle?"

Jaden started, and then his face relaxed into a smile. "Mending. I got off lucky. And you? You look a little worse for wear."

Paul shrugged. "Just fighting off an infection, couple bangs and bumps."

"Good."

"Roger doesn't like you much."

Jaden's dark eyes gleamed. "I'll bet *you* can understand that feeling. You aren't exactly the person any of the Lamberts want to clap eyes on."

Paul grimaced. "True enough. I'm just here until Maddie gets her father moved home."

"Then you go?"

"Then I go." He looked closely at Jaden. "So what are your plans?"

"Same as you. To get Mr. Lambert settled in safely."

"But you think someone is still out to get him?"

"Wrigley's death wasn't an accident."

"So why does Roger think you are involved somehow?"

Jaden folded his arms and stared at Paul, expressionless. "I've no idea."

The nagging suspicion flared again. *I'll bet you do,* he thought grimly, as he watched Jaden disappear down a shadowed corridor.

SIXTEEN

Maddie's back was stiff from sitting in the chair next to her sleeping father. The police officer poked his head in and nodded at her before returning to the hallway. She drew in a deep breath, trying to still the storm of emotion she felt.

It was as if she could still feel her lips against Paul's throat and his warm embrace. His touch comforted her in a way that nothing ever had before. One part of their conversation danced in her mind.

Some things are only God's to know.

There was no way to make sense of what had happened, to know the why of it. Paul hung on to his faith in spite of the bottomless pain, or maybe because he accepted that there were things in this world, agony and heartbreak, that only God understood.

Was it enough to know that God held the pain and suffering in His hands? That there was a loving Father who had a plan so big it could not be fathomed by people like Maddie and Paul? Was that the cure for the anger that threatened to drown her? It did not take away the pain, but it did provide comfort and a way to forgive.

Was she ready to forgive Paul?

Her father's room was dark, the tiny lights from the monitors blinking red and green in the gloom. There was a pervasive smell of disinfectant and the odor of cafeteria food from down the hall. With a start, she realized her father was looking at her.

Her eyes flooded and she found herself unable to say a word. She took his hand and put her cheek on his palm. He stroked her hair, letting her cry until there were no more tears left. Finally, she lifted her head and looked into his face.

"Dad…"

He smiled and his voice sounded hoarse. "Fancy meeting you here, Madison."

She laughed and cried at the same time. "I didn't think we'd get the heart here in time."

"Got that gizmo all installed and it's thumping along like clockwork. No more breathing tube and all the intravenous drugs a man can stand. I'll be right as rain in no time."

A nurse came in and checked her father's vitals. She pressed his feet and ankles and took his temperature.

"How is he?" Maddie asked.

She shot a look over her glasses. "He's doing well, but he still shouldn't be going home tomorrow."

He snorted. "I've hired a nurse to care for me and even a private doctor scheduled to check on me daily. Don't worry. I'll have someone to wake me up every half hour to see if I'm sleeping comfortably."

The nurse didn't smile. Instead, she shook her head at Maddie. "Good luck, Ms. Lambert. You're going to need it to keep this patient in check."

Maddie couldn't help but grin at her stubborn father. His face was creased with fatigue, but more animated than she had seen in months. He was more like the father she'd known before the accident. "I've been so worried about you."

"You weren't the only one worried." His face sobered. "I heard about your plane crash."

"You did? I thought they didn't want to upset you."

"Oh, your sister didn't breathe a word, but I could see on her face something was wrong. I heard the nurses talking about it when they thought I was asleep. I was going to have Tai tell me the details, but the doctors kept him out. Let's hear your story."

She straightened his blanket, wondering how much her father actually knew. She wanted to ask him why he hadn't told her Jaden worked for him, but she feared distressing him. "Don't you think you should rest?"

He huffed. "I've been resting for months. I feel better than I have in years, except for the pain of having my ribs cracked open, and I'm going home tomorrow. I'm strong enough to hear the details. I gathered there was talk that the pilot was drugged."

She nodded.

He grimaced. "The thought that anyone would try to harm you on purpose makes me crazy. Tell me what happened."

Maddie sucked in a breath. "The pilot managed to land us, but he was killed in the crash along with the copilot. We were on our own for a couple of days and somebody took some shots at us."

His voice wobbled. "Maddie, I can't believe you're here, standing next to me."

"Me neither. It was a miracle that we all survived, except for the pilot."

"Who's we?"

She knew it would do no good to try to hide the truth. Her father had the uncanny ability to sniff out a lie. It was part of what made him good at his job. "Tai Jaden, Dr. Wrigley, me…and Paul."

"Paul Ford and Wrigley?"

"Yes."

Her father's eyes narrowed. "Wouldn't surprise me if they

weren't in on a plan together and somebody turned the tables on them."

She shrugged. "I don't know."

"They're only out to save their own skins. They wouldn't think twice about harming you to get to me."

She weighed the decision in her mind before she spoke. "Dad, I know you don't want to hear it, but Paul saved me and probably Tai, too. He lured the shooter away until the rescuers found us."

"That's what he wants you to think, I'm sure. He's got a lot of ground to make up with you." He squeezed her hand. "I hope you're not going to fall for it."

"What?"

He coughed and winced. "Believing him. He wants you to forget what he's done, impress you so we'll drop the suit against him."

"What he did out there on the mountain was not about impressing me." She remembered Paul's face, drawn in pain, blood seeping through his shirt as he struggled through the snow to find her some shelter, and the look of grim determination when he'd hiked to the mountain alone.

It was quiet except for the soft beep of the heart monitor.

Her father spoke very softly. "You still love him, don't you?"

Maddie felt her insides tighten. *Love him? After all that had happened?* Could she still love him, without the past intruding on her emotions? "I don't know."

He let go of her hand, his tone faint but strident. "Maddie, everything I've done since your mother died has been about protecting you girls, sheltering my family from harm. I will not let anyone who hurt us get away unpunished. Do you understand me? Paul will pay and you will get over those feelings that you mistake for love, just like Katie got over Roger."

She thought how harsh her father looked, how hardened. His tone was so bitter it made her want to run out of the room, but it had been only days since he'd had a heart transplant, and it was not good for him to be stressed. Instead she took his hand again. "We can talk more later. Right now, you need to rest."

Bruce Lambert nodded and closed his eyes. "You'll see things more clearly tomorrow," he mumbled.

Maddie was glad when his breathing fell into the rhythm of sleep so he could not see the tears the flowed down her cheeks. She felt numb and exhausted, wishing she could go and sit with Paul in the waiting area.

Instead, she sat on the chair next to her father until sleep overtook her.

In her dream, Maddie was crouched in a dark cave alone. The only sound came from the wind and the driving snow, until a soft crunch echoed from the darkness behind her. She pressed against the cold rock and listened.

The crunching grew louder, along with the sound of breathing. She sought a way to escape, but she was entombed by unforgiving rock.

Maddie's eyes flew open, and for a moment she wondered if she really was back in that terrible cave, fleeing from both a killer and a mountain lion. Reality pressed in upon her and she remembered where she was, in a private hospital room with her father. It was dark and quiet, but her instincts screamed that something was wrong. Heart pounding, she remained still, ears and eyes straining in the darkness.

A shape loomed before her, a figure, bent over her father's bed, pillow in hand.

As Paul rounded the corner after another walk of the floor, he heard Maddie's scream. He ran to Bruce Lambert's room.

Maddie charged out and crashed into him. They both went down in a tangle on the tile floor.

Her body was rigid, shuddering with fear. Paul gripped her arms. "What is it? I heard you scream."

Eyes wild, she looked at him, seemingly unable to form the words. Paul helped her up and she pointed to her father's room. "In there."

They raced toward the room in time to meet the cop who was also panting from his sprint down the hallway. "I got paged to the front desk, but there was nobody on the line. I just saw you both running. What happened?" He didn't wait for an answer, plunging through the door and flipping on the lights, calling for security on his radio as he went.

"What in tarnation do you think you're doing?" he heard Bruce Lambert rasp. "You could have scared me into cardiac arrest."

Paul heaved a gasp of relief. At least her father was all right, judging by the fervor in his chastisement of the cop.

Maddie was still panting, her body shaking all over. "A man. A man holding a pillow. I think he was going to smother Dad. I fell trying to get up and he ran by me."

Paul's mind reeled. He looked wildly around the hall, but there was no sign of the intruder—until he noticed the tiny movement of the stairwell door as it finished closing. He didn't wait to explain, but took off for the stairs, slamming through the door and seeing no one. The sound of feet clattering down the steps echoed against the cement walls and he careened down, hesitating only a moment at each turn to listen.

His breath sounded loud as he raced on, expecting to encounter the man any moment. Ahead was a different noise, close. The sound of hands pushing against the panic bar of the door on the next floor. Paul increased his speed until he was running, ignoring the pain in his back and the leg muscles shuddering with exertion.

He shut off the pain and braced himself to hurtle forward, stopping the guy by hanging on to his ankles if possible. One way or another, the intruder was not getting out of that hospital.

Paul could see the intrusion of light into the corridor from the door opening a few feet ahead of him.

He exploded around the corner just as a crash nearly deafened him. An orderly lay on his back in the threshold, the remains of his tray lunch scattered around him. He clapped a hand to his forehead and groaned. "Some guy nearly killed me."

Paul stopped, struggling to catch his breath. "Are you hurt?"

The orderly sat up and picked some lettuce from his bald head. "Man. I knew exercise was gonna get me one day. I decided to take the stairs down to the atrium to get me a workout, and look what happens?"

"Did you see the guy who knocked you over?"

"Not really. Dark hair is all I remember. I had a lunch tray in my face at the time."

Paul helped the man to his feet and they piled the ruined lunch back on the tray. "Sorry you got caught in the middle."

"You a cop or something?"

Paul shook his head. "No, but they're going to want to talk to you. Why don't you come back upstairs with me?"

"Okay, but I'm takin' the elevator this time."

Paul agreed. His own legs felt like rubber. On the way to the elevator, he ran the situation over in his mind. If the attacker was willing to risk taking action in a public place with police protection, he must be getting desperate. Another thought chilled him to the bone. Maddie had been in that room, probably asleep. The guy had had an easy opportunity to harm her, as well.

They rode to the tenth floor, the orderly still clutching his lunch tray. When they emerged on the correct floor, there were more cops and hospital security milling around. He caught sight of Maddie biting her lip. She broke away from her conversation and ran to him.

He pulled her close and tightened his arms around her, feeling the slam of her heart into her ribs. "The guy got away. How is your father?"

"He's okay. More angry than scared."

"And you?"

She offered a watery grin. "More scared than anything else. I worried you weren't going to catch the guy, and then I worried what would happen if you did."

And she was truly concerned about him. He could feel it in the way her arms stroked his back, in the warmth of her cheek against his chest. He kept her there until a police officer came to get his statement, then he led Maddie to a chair and they sat, knees together.

"Maybe my father is right about leaving here," Maddie said finally. "At home we can protect him. There's an alarm system in the house, and it's hard to get to without being noticed. Jaden will be there, and Katie, Roger and I."

"I don't think it's a good idea. Aside from the fact that your father's body could start to reject the transplant, he's still a target, and you, too, if you're there with him."

"My dad will have round-the-clock medical care and I can take care of myself." The tiny quiver in her voice belied her bravado.

"I know you can, I'm just concerned."

The elevator doors opened again and Jaden stepped out and hastened over to them unsteadily on his wounded ankle, a bag hanging from his shoulder. "What's going on?"

Paul took in his mussed hair and the sheen of perspiration on his brow. "Some trouble. Why are you breathing hard?"

"I was downstairs and I saw the cops arrive. The elevators were full, so I took the stairs. But my ankle wouldn't hold up so I had to resort to the elevator."

"What were you doing downstairs?"

Jaden smiled. "I was working on my laptop, doing some research and getting in order things that I needed to talk to Mr. Lambert about in the morning."

Paul looked at him closely. "It didn't occur to you to go get some sleep?"

He arched an eyebrow. "No, and I guess it didn't occur to you, either."

Maddie sighed. "Someone tried to get to Dad. Did you see anyone running down the stairs?"

Jaden's expression didn't change. "No. I didn't see anyone." He paused. "Actually, I was going over the police report about the accident, the one that injured your father."

At least he avoided mentioning the nieces, Paul thought. "Why are you interested in that?"

He shrugged. "It's my job to be thorough. Your brother said there was another vehicle involved that cut him off, and he overreacted and hit Maddie's father's car."

Paul saw Maddie stiffen. "That's what he said, but no witnesses could corroborate it."

"What if there was someone else there?"

Maddie's mouth pinched in anger. "Mark was driving drunk, he crashed into my father and he was convicted of manslaughter. Those are the facts."

Jaden nodded. "I'm not disputing that. But if there was someone else involved, we've got a new spin on the situation."

Maddie's mouth dropped open. "What spin?"

"The accident might have been an attempt on your father's life."

Maddie groaned.

Paul recalled his brother's insistence that there was another car that awful day. Maddie was right, it didn't absolve his brother from causing the deaths, he wanted to reassure her, but she was interrogating Jaden.

She folded her arms as if she was very cold. "Who do you think is responsible?"

Jaden shook his head. "I don't know yet, but it must be someone with knowledge about what room your father was in."

Paul shook his head. "Plenty of people know that. Most hospital employees could find out with the click of a mouse."

He nodded. "I get the feeling it's someone very close to the situation, maybe even someone who has known your father for a long time."

A police officer joined the group and Jaden introduced himself. "I'm helping with Mr. Lambert's security when he reaches home. Can I go over a few specifics with you?"

The officer nodded and the two men moved away.

Maddie's face was shadowed with fatigue, and she would not meet Paul's eyes.

He considered keeping his thoughts to himself, but the nagging feeling was back. "What do you know about Tai Jaden?"

"Only what I told you. My father trusts him. Why?"

"I heard him talking to Roger downstairs. It sounded like Roger thinks Jaden is involved."

"I don't know how Roger would know that. He left my sister five years ago, quit his job and moved away."

"Maybe he kept in contact with Katie?"

Maddie sighed. "Dad made that difficult. He changed

our phone number and sent back any mail that came from Roger."

Paul wasn't surprised. "Your father isn't big on forgiveness."

"No." Maddie looked so sad that he grabbed both her hands and pressed them to his lips.

That doesn't have to be the way it is, Maddie, he wanted to shout. *We can move on, leave behind the anger and blame.* If he could only see the slightest indication that they could recapture what they used to have.

She turned those bottomless blue eyes on him, and what he saw there instead was hurt, a deep and profound scar left by a tragedy that had cut down to the core of her, kept in place by her father's relentless need for vengeance. She would not be able to cross that river of pain, because she would have to leave her father alone on the other side.

He knew in that moment that things between them, his childish vision of a future with Maddie, was merely self-delusion. He would help her, keep her safe until the security was in place to care for the Lambert family, and then he would go.

"It's okay, Mads. We're going to get through this mess somehow."

The elevator dinged. Paul was surprised to see Detective Burton step out. "You got here fast, detective."

"I was in town anyway. We got confirmation."

Paul felt the foreboding slither up his spine. "Confirmation of what?"

"The bullet that killed Dr. Wrigley came from the same gun that was fired at you two at the crash site."

"So the shooter—" he began.

"Is now officially a murderer."

SEVENTEEN

For a moment, Maddie was completely lost in a whirl of terror. It was real, no coincidences involved. The person who shot at them killed Dr. Wrigley.

She tried to take a steadying breath. "And you think that same person was the one in my father's hospital room?"

Burton shrugged. "That I don't know. You can't give me any descriptive details? Color? Height?"

Maddie shook her head miserably. "No."

"And you?" He looked at Paul. "Nothing?"

"I never saw him."

"Amazing. You chased the guy and you didn't get a glimpse of him?"

Paul sighed. "All I can say is he was pretty tired out by the time he exited the stairwell, judging by the sound of his footsteps."

"Wrigley described the suspect as old. That fits."

Maddie's stomach squeezed. Nothing fit. Nothing at all. Another jolt of terror shook through her. "I've got to call my sister. He could be headed for the house."

Burton nodded. "My guess is he's going to hole up somewhere, but I've already sent a unit to check things out."

She thanked him and pulled out her cell phone while Paul

continued to talk with Burton. Katie answered on the third ring, her voice thick with fatigue.

"Katie," Maddie gasped, suddenly overwhelmed. "Are you okay?"

"Yes, I'm fine. Why?" Her voice edged up in fear. "Is it Dad? Has he taken a turn for the worst?"

"There was an intruder in his room."

"An intruder?"

Maddie wished she could crawl through the phone and hug her sister, ease the panic. "Everyone is okay. Did you activate the alarm?"

"I don't know how. It's just a bunch of buttons."

"Is Roger there?"

"He's staying in the guest house."

"Go wake him up and ask him to set the alarm. He'll know how. He was always a whiz at that stuff."

She hesitated. "I hate to wake him. He really needs his sleep."

Maddie tried to keep her voice calm. "Katie, I know he won't mind you waking him up. Call over to the guest house and ask him to come. There's a cop on the way to check out the grounds, but you need to have the alarm set until they get there."

"Do you really think someone will come here, Maddie?"

She looked at Paul, who stood, arms crossed watching Jaden, deep in thought. "It's best to be prepared."

Maddie made her way past the uniformed officers and into her father's room. It was almost sunrise, and he sat propped up, hands folded neatly over his stomach.

"Did you get any sleep at all, Dad?"

His voice sounded stronger than the day before. "Some. I don't need very much anyway. How about you?"

She sank into a chair. "Oh, Dad. I've never been so scared. What if someone tries again?"

He smiled. "Don't you worry, Madison. I'm a tough old guy, and no one is going to take me down. We'll go home, you, me and Katie, and we'll start over again."

She tried a smile. "The Three Musketeers?"

He patted her hand. "Just like the old days."

Though Maddie continued to smile, she knew he was wrong. Like it or not, Katie and Roger were on amicable terms. Maybe they would never reconcile, yet having him around as a friend might be very helpful for her sister. But their father would never accept it. Just like he would never accept Paul being a part of Maddie's life again.

"Are you thinking about Paul?"

She jumped at her father's voice. "I…"

"You've always been easy to read. You're grateful to him for helping you out, and he's taken full advantage of the opportunity to be close to you, but he has his own agenda. He wants to go back to practicing medicine. He wants to forget his failure in the emergency room."

She looked at her lap.

"And most of all, he wants you to forget that his brother killed your nieces."

Maddie cleared her throat. "I don't think you're right about that. Paul will never forget those facts, and he knows I won't, either."

"Good." Her father's gaze was clear and strong. "Make sure you always remember who your enemies are, Madison."

She held his hand, watching the sunlight filter through the blinds and paint his face in light. He had never forgotten or forgiven anyone who had ever crossed him. He would not show one shred of mercy toward Paul. In spite of the sun, a cold shadow fell over her heart. She adored this man, tried to emulate his work ethic and drive to succeed, loved him for the care he'd showered on Maddie and her sister, followed his path all the years of her life.

But now she saw in him, for the first time, a bitter streak of hatred that sparked in his eyes and expressed itself in the hard lines of his face. Where would she find herself at the sunset of her own life? Walled away from people by nursed grudges, mortared into her own dark place by carefully tended hurts?

She thought of Paul, of his sleepless nights, of the agony he felt at failing, and the simple faith that kept him alive.

Her accusations in the cave came back to her, along with his incredulous reply.

Maddie, tell me you believe I gave up on those little girls.

She did not believe it. Deep down in the innermost mirror of her heart, she knew Paul had done everything he could to save them. The admission flowed out, warming the place where she knew her soul must still linger in spite of the pain. She did not blame Paul anymore. He was right. Some things were only God's to know.

The peace was so tender and soothing that it almost pulled her away completely, but her father's fingers tightened around hers and she opened her eyes to find him staring at her.

"I need you, Madison," he said.

The shock of those words rippled through her. He had never said such a thing before—to anyone, as far as she knew. "I'm right here."

He blinked as if he were seeing her for the first time. "I'm an old man. I've got enough fortune to last for the rest of my life and then some. The only thing that would hurt me now is if I lost you girls."

She felt the tears threaten. "Dad, I'll be here for you. I promise."

He looked away, eyes roving the ceiling. "It's funny, you

know. When I learned they had to take out my heart to give me a new one I worried, just for a moment, that maybe it would take away my feelings, too—all the love stored up inside me." His voice quavered and he cleared his throat. "I realized when I saw you and Katie, my heart isn't inside me anymore anyway, it's walking around inside of you two."

Maddie got up and wrapped her arms gently around her father, tears wetting his blankets. "I love you, Daddy."

"Love you, too, Madison."

She embraced him until the tears ebbed.

"All right now," he said. "You go see what time they're letting me out of this nuthouse."

"Okay." She kissed him and walked to the door. "I just need to do one thing first."

Her heart felt like a lead weight as she went to find Paul in the waiting room. Why did it hurt so much, she wondered? It didn't matter what she wanted, the feelings she had for him. Her place was with her father, just as she'd always known it was. It was not fair to Paul or Katie or anyone else to keep him close, constantly reopening wounds inside all of them. Paul deserved a clean break, and she could at least give him that.

Though her body screamed at her every step of the way, she walked over to him and looked into his eyes. "Paul, I need to tell you something."

Paul saw the warring emotions on Maddie's face. He wanted to ease her discomfort. Instead he braced himself and nodded for her to continue.

"My mind is all jumbled up. It seems so unreal, everything that's happened." She stammered to a stop.

He gave her a moment to collect herself before he spoke. "You've been through a lot. Tell me what you need to say."

She straightened and blurted it out. "I want you to leave."

He'd known it was coming, but the words cut deep anyway. "I understand you don't want to upset your father."

"That's not it. He knows you're here anyway, and I told him how much you'd helped me."

Paul gaped. "You did? That took a lot of courage."

Maddie shrugged. "It's the truth, whether he likes it or not. The thing is, he needs me and Katie more than ever. We're all he has left."

And you're all I have left, Maddie. I can't give my heart to anyone else. With a great effort, he stayed quiet and let her continue.

"My dad, he's hardened inside and he sees people as friends or in the enemy camp, and he never changes his mind."

"And I'm always going to be the enemy?"

She bit her lip. "Yes. It's not right, I see that now, but that's the way he is. I—I think I was beginning to be like that, too, letting the anger turn me into someone else."

He leaned forward and took her hand. "But things have changed?"

Tears sparkled in her blue eyes and she squeezed his hand. "I believe you did everything humanly possible to save my nieces."

The emotion was so thick in his throat he could not answer. They were the sweetest words he had ever heard.

She took a breath. "I lost sight of things for a while, I forgot that God is in charge and that sometimes we're not going to know the whys and wherefores. I wanted to blame someone. I wanted the situation to be as black-and-white as it was for my father." She gripped his fingers. "I'm sorry, Paul. I'm sorry for the things I said."

He wanted to take her in his arms and kiss her tears away, but he sensed she had more to say. "Mads, I'm sorry, too. I'm so sorry for my brother, for loaning him the car—" he pressed a kiss to her fingers "—for not being able to save them."

"I know, I know. I'm going to be all right now, Paul. I really think so, but we're not going to get back what we had. I can't abandon my father and sister, and you can't be a part of a family that will always despise you."

She was crying hard now and he stood, scooping her into his arms.

"I can't leave you now. You're in danger," he said, wiping her tears away.

"I have Jaden and Roger. The police are involved. There's nothing you can do that they can't."

His voice came out in a whisper. "They can't love you the way that I do, Mads. I never stopped. Tell me you love me, too, and we'll find a way to make it work."

She looked at him for a long moment and then kissed him, wrapping her arms around his neck.

He felt the silk of her hair against his face, the tenderness in her mouth, tasted the salt of her tears. He sensed something else there, besides the sweetness that made him dizzy. He sensed in her kiss the finality of the goodbye.

She pulled away, traced a finger down his cheek, eyes searching as if to memorize every inch of his face, then she turned and walked away.

He watched her go, his body numb and cold. From this day on he would see her only in court dates, perhaps. She would be cool and professional, sitting next to her father and sister as they brought the suit against him. They would be strangers, and she would go on living through joy and sorrows, growing and changing in ways he'd never know.

But she'd given him one thing. She told him she did not blame him, and it was a gift for herself, too, to let go of the bitterness that twisted her heart and turned her away from God. He wished he could embrace the joy of that transformation, but he was sure at that moment, that his greatest chance at joy just walked away.

Goodbye, Mads. I'll always love you.

There was nothing to be done then but call for a taxi to the nearest airport. While he waited in the lobby for his ride, he saw an ambulance pull up. The attendants asked at the desk for Bruce Lambert. A cop waited outside.

It eased the tension in his gut that lurked under the pain. Maddie would be safe and protected. He was glad the police were involved, at least initially. If Jaden was up to something, it would be hard to accomplish under close scrutiny.

His cab arrived after a while and he got in. As they pulled away, he saw the medics loading Bruce Lambert into the ambulance and Maddie and Jaden watching the whole process. Though she didn't know Paul was in the cab that passed her, she turned her face to the cloudy sky. Watery sunlight showed the pain drawn there, and he felt a similar agony in his own heart.

He prayed that after he was gone, and the whole lawsuit business was over, she would find happiness again, even if it could not be with him.

The cabbie chattered nonstop as they drove along the storm-slicked roads, hitting pockets of traffic that slowed their journey. It was not until lunchtime that he made it to the terminal. He found himself checking his watch, wondering about Maddie. The drive to the Lambert estate would take several hours, so she and her father had probably not arrived yet.

Let her go, Paul.

He focused on buying a ticket and another ridiculous, gritty adventure novel to pass the hour until his flight took off. The steely Mitch, former navy SEAL, did not hold his attention. His gaze drifted to the terminal window, where, outside, planes taxied to and fro on the tarmac. He should be feeling some post-traumatic shock, he supposed, about boarding another plane so soon after surviving a crash, but he didn't feel anything but cold despair.

Time would heal the wounds, he told himself. At least in his arrogance, that's what he would have told the grieving families he worked with. Now he was not convinced. Time might scab over the wounds, but they would always be there, running as deep as his love for Maddie.

Hunger gnawed at his belly and he realized he hadn't eaten since the packet of candy the night before. A small kiosk at the far end of the terminal offered sandwiches and coffee, so he headed there. A man was in front of him in line, close to Paul's age, clutching the coffee he'd just bought. When he turned, something caused him to stagger and the coffee cup dropped to the floor, splashing Paul's feet.

The man looked at him, eyes wide. "I'm really sorry about that."

"No problem," Paul said, grabbing a paper napkin to wipe his shoes and the puddle of coffee. The man bent to help and swayed. Paul reached out a hand to steady him.

"You okay?"

The man's face reddened. "People always think I've been drinking, but it's Parkinson's."

Paul nodded. The insidious disease that caused muscle stiffness and tremors could strike the young as well as the old. He wished he could offer some comfort to the man. "Can I buy you a new coffee? I'm just waiting for a flight. We can down some caffeine together."

He offered a smile. "No, thanks." The clerk handed him another cup of coffee. "But I appreciate the kindness. It's not easy having people always think you're a drunk."

He walked away and Paul watched him plod across the terminal, coffee clutched in his hand.

What would it be like to be constantly mistaken for inebriated?

Something fired in Paul's brain.

Or old?

He was so lost in thought he didn't hear the cashier ask him until she tapped his shoulder. "Can I get you something?"

Paul's hunger was suddenly gone. "No, thanks. Changed my mind." He hurried back to his seat, dialing as he went. Maddie wasn't answering. Jaden would have to do. He pulled up Jaden's number and clicked.

The phone rang but there was no answer. He checked his watch. It was now close to two o'clock. They were probably just arriving, getting Bruce settled in under a nurse's supervision.

He sat back and tried to think it through. He was likely imagining the whole thing anyway. Trying to find ways to be the big hero.

He'd had his chance at that and failed. Maddie wanted him out of her life. She would not appreciate his wild theory, that was probably as unlikely as navy SEAL Mitch shutting down a nuclear reactor all on his own.

Paul sighed. *Just get on the plane and do what she asked you to do.*

Still, he could not forget the man who'd stumbled and dropped his coffee.

Paul found himself unable to sit still any longer. He paced the floor, dialing Jaden two more times with no answer.

He could phone the police.

And probably be dismissed as crazy, or trying to interfere, by the suspicious Detective Burton.

Besides, the whole idea was ludicrous, a product of Paul's imagination, a manifestation of his need to be involved in Maddie's life.

Let her go, Paul.

The announcement came for him to board his flight. He

took his place in line and the lady extended a hand to take his ticket. "Welcome, Dr. Ford. Have a nice flight."

He glanced out the window one last time before he entered the corridor to the plane.

Let her go, his mind said, but he listened to his heart instead, reversing directions and running for the rental-car counter.

EIGHTEEN

Maddie expected to feel a sharp surge of relief as they pulled onto the large, circular drive at her father's stately mansion, but she still felt disconnected, adrift, as if she'd left something important behind.

The kiss, her goodbye, still felt so real on her lips, the tenderness in him which flowed out so clearly, so potently across her senses. He was gone by now, flying home to a life without her. She swallowed hard and forced a smile for the nurse, whose name was Carolyn. Katie emerged from the house, followed by Roger, who stayed back in the shadows while they watched, as the patient was moved carefully up the gleaming oak stairs, croaking orders all the while.

"I'm glad you got here," Katie said, after squeezing Maddie close as Roger joined them. "There's a storm coming, maybe some snow."

Jaden entered and, after a curt greeting, headed for the stairs.

Roger shot out a hand. "Where are you going?"

"I need to talk to Mr. Lambert."

Roger frowned. "What is it with you? The man just crossed the threshold. He deserves a chance to settle in."

Jaden's eyes were dark and expressionless. "I need to ask him something."

Roger looked as if he was about to lash out, so Maddie intervened. "In a while. The nurse said she wants to get my father comfortable and make sure his levels are where they need to be. I don't think it would be a good idea to bother him now."

Jaden shrugged and sat purposefully on a leather chair in the front room. "I'll wait."

Maddie nodded, thinking about Paul's suspicions about the man. Her father trusted Jaden, so Maddie did, too; but she decided to make it a point to be with her father whenever Jaden was. "Dad thought you would be comfortable staying in the guest house."

There were three bedrooms there, so even with Roger's addition there would be plenty of places to sleep.

Jaden nodded. "Fine. I'll wait here until he's ready to talk."

Maddie nodded and went upstairs to check in. Carolyn, the nurse, smiled cheerfully.

"He's all tucked in, but I think the drive might have tired him out."

He snorted. "I can talk for myself."

Maddie intervened and showed Carolyn to the adjoining room where she would be staying. "I'll sit with him while you get unpacked." When she returned she found her father struggling to stay awake.

"Hate to admit that she's right."

"It's okay to take a nap."

He nodded and closed his eyes.

"Dad, before you sleep, what can you tell me about Tai Jaden?"

"Good man," he mumbled. "I'd trust him with my life."

As her father drifted off she wondered if he'd put his trust in the right man.

Her thoughts wandered back to Paul as she walked to the

huge bay windows that overlooked the gardens. The sky was thick with clouds, the wind bending the slender, bare branches of the trees below. Another storm coming in, cold and icy. She hoped Paul's flight was not affected by the weather. The ache in her stomach returned and she settled in an armchair near her father's bed. His steady, rhythmic breathing reminded her he needed her more than Paul did. The amazing machine the doctors had put inside his chest would only save him as long as his body did not reject it. He needed sleep and rest and his daughters nearby.

She tried to put Paul out of her mind, but he remained there, his gray eyes and laughter, until she, too, fell asleep— to be startled awake several hours later by the nurse.

"What time is it? It's so dark." Maddie asked, rubbing a hand over her gritty eyes.

"Just after five. You looked so tired I thought I'd let you sleep. Mr. Lambert told me he sent the cook home for the evening to beat the storm, but she left sandwiches and salads in the kitchen."

Maddie nodded. "Where is everyone?"

"I'm not sure. Mr. Jaden came in, but your father was asleep, so he went out again. He said he was going to go for a drive. I saw your sister in the kitchen about a half hour ago, wrapping a sandwich to take out to the guest house."

Katie would want to be sure Roger had something to eat. "I'll go talk to her. Will you stay with Dad?"

"Of course. That's why I'm here." Carolyn began smoothing the bed linens as Maddie went out.

In the kitchen, she helped herself to a sandwich even though she didn't feel hungry. The storm rattled the windows. She wondered if Katie had thought to bring an umbrella. As she chewed, the last of the sunlight disappeared and the early winter night was upon them.

Across a small hill, she could see the guest house, lights adding comfort in the gloom. Fat raindrops began to spatter the windows. She picked up the kitchen phone and dialed her sister's cell to see if she wanted Maddie to bring her an umbrella.

Katie picked up on the first ring. "Maddie—"

The phone went dead.

"Katie? Did you hang up?" She redialed but received only a busy signal for her trouble.

Probably in a few seconds her sister would call back. She began to pace the marble floor, waiting for the ring. When the phone remained silent, Maddie called again. Still no answer.

Grabbing a raincoat and umbrellas from the hall closet, she let herself out the front, locking the door behind her. The police had checked the property when they arrived and found nothing amiss, but it made her feel better to turn the bolt securely. Maybe it was the moan of the wind and the past that put her on edge, pulling and tearing at her umbrella until she gave up and closed it. Freezing rain drove into her face as she crossed the dark lawn. Even the moon was hidden, and she wished she'd thought to bring a flashlight. Pushing forward, head bent against the storm, she made it to the front step of the cottage.

She used the brass knocker. "Roger? Katie? It's Maddie."

No answer.

She knocked again, as hard as she could, until the door finally opened and she felt a surge of relief.

Roger stood there, coat in hand. "Oh, hi, Maddie. What brings you out in the storm?"

"Katie was bringing you a sandwich. I thought she might need an umbrella on the way back."

"Katie?" He shook his dark head. "Haven't seen her."

"What?" Maddie's heart lurched. "I thought she was coming here. I called her cell, but we were cut off."

He frowned. "Really? She must have gone somewhere else. Are you sure she isn't in the main house?"

"I guess she could be. Can I use the phone and call her cell again?"

He stepped aside and ushered her in. "Of course. I'm going to get a flashlight. It looks like we might lose power soon. Be right back."

She picked up the phone and dialed again, but was not able to get through. A prickle of unease danced up her spine. She thought something scratched at the window behind her, but when she spun around there was nothing there, nothing at all.

Except the plastic-wrapped sandwich sitting innocently on the counter.

Paul felt stiff from the long journey. Each mile brought only more confusion. What was he doing driving back to the Lambert estate on a whim? He was probably totally wrong, and his arrival would throw the family into even more chaos. If he'd been able to get Jaden on the phone, he might have felt better about the whole thing. At least he'd had enough courage to leave a message for Detective Burton.

He swerved to avoid a branch that had blown onto the road. Even the moon seemed to have given up, leaving him driving along in darkness. But as much as he tried to talk himself into turning around, he found himself moving steadily toward the Lambert estate, the tension inside growing with each mile.

It was probably complete coincidence. Wrigley said the shooter was old because he moved slowly, unsteadily. The man Paul had pursued down the stairwell had run like someone fatigued or drunk. But what if the killer wasn't old or tired? What if he was merely manifesting a disease, like Huntington's?

Paul had encountered only a half-dozen cases in his career but he knew the brutal facts. It was a disorder which hit in the prime of life, causing nerve cells in the brain to degenerate. It sometimes caused slow, uncontrolled movements and an unsteady gait. Medicine therapies offered help up to a point.

He'd only seen Roger standing still or sitting, except for the confrontation with Jaden when he'd stumbled.

But it was so ridiculous, it couldn't be true. What motive could he have for wanting to destroy Bruce Lambert and Maddie in the process?

He recalled the most hideous symptom that sometimes manifested in advanced cases.

Madness.

He pushed the gas pedal harder until the phone rang.

Detective Burton's voice surged into the car as Paul put him on speakerphone.

"Ford? Is that you?"

"Yes, detective. Did you get my message?"

"Yes, and I have to admit I figured you were getting some sort of thrill out of playing cop. We run into that all the time."

Paul heard the undercurrent in the man's tone. "What did you find out?"

"Roger Brown, Katie's former husband, worked for a company that chartered jets called AirTime. He was their accountant."

Paul tensed. "Tell me."

"Bruce Lambert knew the owner. The owner became aware of some discrepancies and asked Lambert to investigate unofficially. Roger didn't know his father-in-law was looking into things."

"Until Mr. Lambert found out Roger was stealing money?"

"The whole thing was kept on the down low. Lambert said he'd handle everything if the owner wouldn't press charges. Probably didn't want his daughter embarrassed."

Paul groaned. He could only imagine how Mr. Lambert had handled things with Roger. Whatever he'd said resulted in Roger dropping out of Katie's and the children's lives, and leaving Katie to believe he'd had an affair with another woman. "If I had to guess, I'd say he told Roger to disappear or he'd make sure he spent the rest of his life in jail."

Burton grunted. "So, when he heard the old man was on death's door, he figured he'd pay off the copilot to set down somewhere and snatch the heart? Rejoin his wife and enjoy the Lambert fortune for the rest of his days?"

"I don't know, but we have to get there before he harms Mr. Lambert or Maddie."

"I've got units rolling, but it will take us a while to get there. What's your ETA?"

Paul gunned the motor. "Fifteen minutes."

"Wait there until my cops arrive. Do you hear me, Ford? The guy's murdered Wrigley and brought down a plane. Do not go in there without the cops."

Paul clicked off the phone without answering.

The only thought on his mind was Maddie.

Terror surged through Maddie's body. The sandwich proved Katie had come and Roger was lying. She didn't understand the reasons, but she knew deep down that something was very wrong. The only thing to do was find Katie and get back to the house. She eased the kitchen phone off the cradle and dialed 9-1-1.

There was no dial tone.

She stared at the receiver in her hand as the ice trickled through her veins.

Roger came back. "No phone? Must be the storm." He held a mag light in his hands.

She nodded. "Yes. Yes, I'll go back to the main house for more flashlights."

As she scurried toward the door, Roger stepped in front of her. His face was haggard, eyes gleaming with a feverish light. "Stay here. With Katie."

"Where *is* Katie, Roger?"

He reached out and grabbed her wrist. Though his body looked frail, his grip was strong. She tried to twist away, to kick out, but he folded her arm behind her and shoved her down the hall, talking in her ear.

"The Lamberts are always meddling where they aren't wanted, making trouble where there doesn't need to be any. I was trying to make a future for us, me and Katie, without any of the dirty Lambert money. A self-made man, someone your father would respect, but did he give me the chance?" Roger hissed in her ear. "No, he got me fired and made Katie think I cheated on her."

Maddie's mind whirled. "You were stealing money?"

Roger shoved her. "Borrowing. But Old Man Lambert ruined all that. He sent me away, so I came back to even the score. Should have been over with the car crash."

Maddie stiffened. "Did you cause the car accident?" The horror washed over her in waves. "Oh, Roger. Your children. Your girls."

He squeezed her arm so tight she thought her bones would break. "I didn't know they were in the car. All I did was force some poor schlub into Lambert's car."

She could hardly mouth the words. "But the girls, your daughters."

He stumbled, moving close enough for her to see the bead

of sweat forming on his brow. "Lambert killed my daughters when he sent me away. It wasn't me, Maddie. It wasn't me."

She felt the bile rise in her throat—for what he had done, for what they all had lost. He shoved her into the back bedroom, but Maddie still saw no sign of her sister. She tried to play for time. "Did you crash the plane, Roger?"

He gave her a shove that sent her sprawling on the bed. She rolled over, scrambling to the far side, looking into his glittering eyes.

"It was supposed to be the perfect crime. Paid off a pilot I used to know. Guy's got a gambling problem so he needed to disappear anyway. He was supposed to knock out the pilot, land in a spot I picked out, grab the heart and meet me. Only something went wrong." He shook his head. "I figured after that crash there would be no survivors. You could have knocked me over when I saw you four come out of that cave."

Maddie remembered the way the man in the ski mask had stiffened at the sight of them. "So you had to try and kill us then, because we might identify you later."

"No. Only that snob of a doctor could identify me face-to-face because I got careless, so I had to take care of him. I just wanted to make sure the heart wouldn't make it to the old man, so there'd be no way he could keep me out of Katie's life any longer."

Maddie stared at him, the insanity shimmering on his face, his head jerking, as if an electric current ran through his body. It would do no good, she knew, to try to make him see reality, but maybe she could reason with him, talk him out of whatever he was planning.

"You don't have to go through with this. We can get you some help. People will understand why you were upset with my father. Don't make it worse, Roger. Think about Katie. You love her, don't you?"

His eyes flickered for a moment before he grabbed her wrist again. "I'm going to fix everything, for Katie, too. You'll see. It's all going to be okay."

She struggled as he pushed her toward the closet, causing him to fall to one knee, but still his viselike grip did not loosen, and he regained his footing. Reaching into her pocket, he removed her house keys and then pulled a wooden wedge from under the bottom of the door and propelled her into the dark space.

She heard Roger shove the wedge under the door frame and then his footsteps died away.

Paul pulled up at the estate. The main house was shrouded in darkness, except for lights in the upstairs windows. He checked his watch. Only a little after seven, far too early for the whole house to have turned in for the night. The paved circular driveway was slick, and cold rain snaked down the back of his neck as he headed for the front door.

Quietly, he tried to turn the stately doorknobs. Locked.

He headed around the side of the house. Rounding the corner, he nearly fell over a crumpled body, half tucked under the soggy shrubs. It was Tai Jaden, his face a wash of blood.

Paul checked for a pulse and found one, steady and reassuring. He tried to rouse Jaden with no success, so he unzipped his jacket and covered the man with it as best he could. "I'll be back for you soon," he whispered, part of him wondering if he could deliver on his promise.

Roger was determined to kill Bruce Lambert and anyone else who got in his way. It seemed he was no longer concerned about concealing his crimes, and Paul knew the disease had ravaged whatever rational thoughts Roger might have had. Where was Maddie? Was she in the house, unaware that her brother-in-law was on his way to kill her father?

Rain-soaked and fighting a desperate fear for Maddie, he followed the flagstone path to the porch entrance. The door was open, swinging in the wind.

Paul took a breath and hurried into the house. The lamp near the brick fireplace glowed faintly in the darkness. When his eyes adjusted, he moved toward the staircase.

Where are you, Roger?

As if in answer to his question, the lamp suddenly went out—then the light on the stairway, and finally the glow from the upstairs was extinguished.

NINETEEN

Maddie heard a soft cry as she was propelled into the closet. Her sister clutched at her, fingers ice-cold. "Oh, Maddie. It's Roger. He's crazy. He's crazy."

Maddie hugged her sister. "Honey, I'm so sorry."

"I found Roger cleaning a rifle. He started babbling. He... the accident. My girls, my babies." Her sobs wracked her body so hard her sister's shoulders shuddered. "When he came back to help after the plane crash, I thought we might be able to be friends again, but he's crazy. He's going to kill Dad."

Katie's eyes were round and wild in the dark. Maddie kept her voice calm. "We've got to get out of here. Do you have your phone?"

"No, he took it from me."

"We'll have to force the door."

"I tried before, but he's wedged it."

Maddie pulled Katie to her feet. Katie grimaced. "I think I twisted my ankle trying to kick it in."

"Maybe with two of us." They pushed and slammed at the door until they were breathless, but the sturdy wood wouldn't budge. Maddie felt something akin to panic. Roger was going to kill her father if she didn't find a way out of this closet.

Looking up, she remembered a time long ago, when they

were children, a game of hide-and-seek, where Maddie had found the ultimate hiding place.

"There's a panel up there, an access to the attic. I hid there once, remember?"

Katie sighed. "I remember, but how is that going to help? There's no way out of the attic."

"There's a small opening covered by a screen, for ventilation. We had a raccoon family that got in when we were kids. That's how I got the idea to hide there. I watched the workmen go up into the attic to fix the damage. Give me a boost."

Katie cupped her hands and Maddie clawed at the opening in the ceiling, finding, at last, a small handle. She grabbed it and pulled the hatch down, revealing a folding set of wooden stairs. Scrambling up, she scuttled into the cold air of the attic. Eyes barely able to function, she found what she was looking for, a small rectangular grate at the far side.

"I'm going to climb out of here and get help," she called down to her sister.

Katie whimpered from below. "Please don't confront Roger, Maddie. He's insane. The children…"

Her voice broke off into sobs again, and it took all Maddie's strength not to climb back down to comfort her sister. "I'll get help. Be brave, okay?"

She didn't wait for an answer, instead she walked carefully along the exposed beams until she came to the grate. It was securely fastened to prevent any return rodent visitors. Her heart sank. Frantically, she looked around for something to use. Her eyes caught upon a set of golf clubs. She grabbed one and began to hammer at the slats.

When she thought her trembling muscles would cooperate no longer, one of the slats let go and she dropped the club and pulled at it with all her might. The slat came loose along with several others until she'd cleared a small hole. Kicking the remaining slats loose, she poked her head through the opening. It revealed an eight-foot drop, straight down into the shrubbery.

She could find no rope or even blankets to tie together to lower herself down.

Only an eight-foot drop into darkness.

Her hands prickled with fear, her legs grew wobbly as she pulled herself into the opening. In spite of her fear of falling, a greater terror surged through her—the fact that her father might be murdered at any moment.

She sucked in a deep breath and knew what she had to do.

God, help me do it for Katie and Dad.

Though it had been a very long time since she'd spoken to Him, she had a feeling of peaceful certainty which gave her a sense of calm. No matter what happened, she wasn't in it alone.

After the deepest breath she could manage, she let go and dropped into the night.

Paul knew Roger was in the basement turning off the power to the house. That gave him a few minutes, maybe less, to make it upstairs. He hurtled toward the massive staircase, taking the steps two at a time, until he got to the upper hallway. He had no idea which room was occupied by Maddie's father, until he saw the door at the end open and a lady's face peer out. It must be the nurse.

He ran, catching her just as she started to slam the door. Pushing his way in, he turned the lock behind him.

The nurse's eyes were wide with fear. She grabbed the nearest object, the water pitcher, and raised it threateningly. "Stay back."

"I'm here to help. There's a killer in the house on his way up here."

She gaped. "What are you talking about?"

Paul tried to keep his voice calm. "You've got to hide." His eyes swept the room. "Does that door lead to an adjoining room?"

She nodded, pitcher still raised.

"Go and lock yourself in. Hurry."

Her glance swept to Bruce Lambert, who had begun to stir on the bed. "I can't leave my patient."

"I'll take care of him." She didn't move. Paul felt like shouting, but he managed to control it. "If you don't leave, then you'll both be dead."

The nurse put the pitcher down and backed away. Before she left, Paul hissed at her, "Where's Maddie?"

The nurse whispered back. "I don't know. I think she might have gone to the guest house. I saw her walking across the lawn about a half hour ago."

Paul felt a wave of dark fear ripple through his body. Maddie. Had she confronted Roger? Was she lying injured somewhere?

A gasp from the bed took him from his panicked thoughts. Bruce Lambert sat up, eyes brimming with hatred. "What are you doing here?"

"There's no time to explain. You've got to do what I say."

Lambert shook his head. "I'll do no such thing. Your brother killed my granddaughters and you watched them die. I don't know how you got in here, but I'll see you in jail if it's the last thing I do." He heaved in a breath to shout for help when Paul stepped forward, and pressed a hand over the man's mouth.

"Mr. Lambert, you have your whole life ahead of you to hate me, but right now, you're going to do what I say."

Wet branches stabbed at Maddie as she fell into the shrubbery. The breath whooshed out of her at impact, but she didn't give herself time to recover before she clawed her way out of the foliage and began to run toward the main house, which was now cloaked in darkness. Was she too late? She pounded against the front door. Locked.

She tore around the side of the house toward the porch entrance, when hands grabbed at her. She screamed and nearly fell, until Jaden steadied her. He looked ghastly, as if he could hardly keep his footing.

"Jaden. What happened?"

"It's Roger. By the time I figured it out, it was too late. He attacked me as I made for the house to warn your father."

Her breath caught. "Too late? Has he—"

Jaden held up his hand. "I don't know. I got the police on my cell. They're about five minutes away." He bent over and took a deep breath as if he was about to collapse.

A horrifying realization came over her as she steadied him. "Jaden, is that Paul's jacket?"

"Yes. He came back. He went to try and save your father."

She closed her eyes against an onslaught of dizziness. Paul. She turned to run.

Jaden shot out a hand to stop her. "You can't go in there. Roger is armed, I'm sure. The police will be here soon."

"I've got to." She ran a few steps before Jaden called out again.

"This isn't what your father would want."

She paused for only a moment. "This time it doesn't matter what my father wants."

Paul had less than a minute to carry out his plan, and crouch next to the bedroom door, before he heard Roger's unsteady tread on the stairs.

There was the sound of the door handle rattling and a low voice that chilled him, whispering through the crack. "Old

Man Lambert? Are you in there? It's time for a visit from your long-lost son-in-law."

Paul knew what would happen next. He turned away, covering his face as the bullets exploded into the wooden door, splintering the lock into bits. His ears rang from the noise, and the shooting continued until Roger kicked the ruined panel aside.

He entered the room, unaware of Paul in his hiding place.

"Now, old man. It's time for me to take my rightful place in the family. You thought you could cut me out of Katie's life after you took my children away. It was your fault they died, old man," he said as he approached the bed, gun leveled. "How was I supposed to know you had my girls in the backseat? You were supposed to die, not them."

He paused and aimed the weapon. "So now it's time for you to go."

The shots split the night as he fired round after round into the bed.

Maddie was on her way to the stairs when she heard the shots. Each one seemed to drill right into her heart. Her father. Paul. The nurse. They could all be dead. What would she find when she reached the bedroom?

She should turn around and run. Wait for the police, instead of walk into a room with a crazed shooter.

But Paul's voice echoed in her memory, the love in his face and the tender hands that caressed her so many times. Paul loved her in the pure, unselfish way God intended for a man and woman. She meant so much to him that he would die to save her and her father.

After the bitter anger they'd heaped on him. The weight she'd added to his grief with her own blame and condemnation.

The thoughts whirled in her mind as she plunged up the steps. Crashes and groans rang through the corridor, and the lights flicked on again, just as she crossed the threshold. Paul and Roger slammed to the floor, both grappling for a hold on the gun. Roger's eyes were wild, his mouth set into a grimace. Paul was the stronger of the two, but Maddie knew the plane crash had weakened him.

She looked frantically for something, anything she could use as a weapon to help. The gun fired and she screamed, the bullet knocking a hole in the wall near her head.

Paul shouted, "Maddie, get out of here."

Abandoning her efforts to find a weapon, she grabbed Roger by his feet and held on.

He kicked at her, but she wrapped her hands around his ankles, and the distraction caused him to momentarily loosen his grip on the gun. Paul managed to knock it away. The weapon skittered across the floor. Roger thrashed violently and Maddie was thrown back. Jaden staggered in, stepped over her and joined Paul, throwing his weight on Roger to pin him while Paul secured his hands.

Booted feet sounded on the stairs and she knew the police must have arrived.

Maddie scrambled to her feet, sides heaving, and her eyes were drawn to the ruined bed. She did not want to see, did not want to know the awful truth of what lay underneath those bullet-riddled sheets.

"Oh Dad. Oh Dad," she heard herself say.

Paul called to her, but she did not understand the words.

Her father moaned. Could he still be alive? Could he have been given yet another miracle from God?

She eased closer, fingers grasping the corner of the sheets. She was trying to summon the courage to pull it back, when Paul caught her hand.

"He's okay."

She thought he'd gone mad. "How can you know that?"

Paul bent over. He grabbed hold of something underneath and pulled her father out from under the foot of the bed.

His face was ghastly pale, but his eyes sparked, full of life in spite of the discomfort he must have felt.

"Dad?" She could hardly see him through the tears. "How…?"

The nurse joined them, and with Paul and Jaden's help, got him into a reclining chair.

Her father cleared his throat, sweat filming his face. "In a minute. Where's Katie?"

Maddie tried several times before the words came out. "She's locked in a closet in the guest house."

Jaden nodded, turned and left. Police officers swarmed the room and cuffed Roger, pulling him to his feet and out, but Maddie hardly noticed, lost in the joy of seeing her father alive.

The nurse fussed over her patient until Maddie's father waved her away. "I'm fine, in spite of the rough treatment I was given by this man." He pointed a finger at Paul. "You shouldn't be in my house."

"Dad…"

Her father stopped her, his eyes riveted on Paul. "Regardless of Roger's involvement, your brother was driving drunk and killed my granddaughters."

Paul stood straight without moving. "Yes, sir."

"He will be in jail for a long time, which is what he deserves."

"Yes, sir."

"And you came into my house and ignored my express demands for you to leave, pulling me out of my bed and shoving me none too gently to the floor."

Paul nodded. "Yes, sir, I did."

Her father eyed him for a while. "And you said to me, if I remember correctly, 'You're the only person here, and that makes you my patient. I've never turned my back on a patient yet, and I'm not about to start now.'" He squinted at Paul. "Did I get that right?"

"I believe so."

Her father's tone changed. "And I believe that I have misjudged you, Dr. Ford. The man who dragged me from my bed, is not a man who would turn his back on two small children in need, is he?"

Maddie felt her eyes fill, and saw the gleam of moisture in Paul's.

"No, sir, he isn't," Paul said, as Maddie took his hand.

"All right then. We will sit down and talk more about this soon. Right now, I've got to make sure Katie is all right, and see about getting a new bed."

The nurse moved closer and began to check the old man over, in spite of his objections.

Maddie pulled Paul away to the adjoining room. She examined his face closely. "Are you hurt?"

Paul looked tired, but more at peace than she had ever seen him. "No, Mads. Are you?"

She shook her head. "Nothing serious, except…" Her thickening throat choked off the words.

"What is it?"

"Oh Paul." The words clogged her throat.

"It's all over. Everything is all right now."

She turned away. "No, no it's not. I almost lost my father, and what's worse, I almost lost myself…and you. When the girls died, I turned into someone else, someone I didn't even recognize."

"Grief can do that."

She whirled to face him. "But it wasn't fair to hurt you

like that, when you already felt responsible. Was that really me, Paul? Did I really do that?"

He pulled her close. "It was a bad time for all of us, and you needed to be angry."

A deep longing swirled through her heart. She clutched at him, desperate to make him understand. "Can you ever forgive me for blaming you? I let my father's rage feed something inside me, and I feel so ashamed." She looked at her feet, suddenly unable to meet his gaze.

He was silent for a long moment. "I just need to know one thing, Mads. Do you love me?"

Tears washed down her face and her voice came out a ragged whisper. "Yes. I've always loved you and I always will." She took a breath and forced out the question she was most afraid to ask. "After all that's happened, do we still have a future together?" She held her breath.

He caressed her cheek and tipped her chin up. A faint smile quirked his lips. "Now that I look at you, Mads, you seem really tired, in my professional opinion." He kissed her temple and she felt her pulse flutter.

Her blue eyes were clear, there was no anger there anymore, no blame.

"Really?" she whispered.

"Yes. My diagnosis is fatigue."

The next kiss landed on her other temple, then her forehead. She felt dizzy with the sensation.

Paul stroked her hair, her cheeks, her temples. "What you should do is take a long vacation. Maybe to Yosemite."

Her heart pounded a joyful rhythm. "Why there?"

"Because the snow is great and they've even got a little wedding chapel."

She did not think she would ever feel joy again after the accident but now her heart was filled to overflowing. They could not go back to what they were before, but God was giving them a way to go forward, to become something different, together. "Are you sure, Paul?"

He smiled, his lips playing over hers. "Oh yes. Trust me, Mads. I'm a doctor."

* * * * *

Dear Reader,

The truth can look so different, depending on the viewpoint. Maddie Lambert is certain that her former fiancé, Dr. Paul Ford, let her nieces die to save his own brother. Her belief is reinforced by her father's relentless need for vengeance. It will take a plane crash and a deadly assassin to make Maddie question her version of the truth.

So many times, the tragedies and disappointments of this world lead us to build our own truths that can wall us away from others, or bury us under bitter piles of resentment. I hope, dear reader, that you will come away from reading *Turbulence* with a lifting of your spirit, a sweet reminder of the ultimate truth. As St. Augustine said, "God loves each of us as if there were only one of us."

Thank you for taking time out of your life to read my book. I'd love to hear any thoughts or comments you would like to share. Feel free to contact me via my website at www.danamentink.com anytime.

Blessings,

Dana Mentink

QUESTIONS FOR DISCUSSION

1. Maddie believes in the opening chapters that her past with Paul will be an "impossible wedge" between them forever. Do you know of relationships where there is seemingly no hope of reconciliation?

2. What is your initial impression of Paul Ford?

3. Dr. Wrigley describes Maddie as an unstable, grief-blinded woman. What do you think of his assessment?

4. Paul says love and anger aren't compatible. Do you agree?

5. Have you ever been in a dangerous situation where you were entirely on your own, with no way to summon help? How did you handle it?

6. Her nieces' deaths kindled an "impenetrable fear" inside Maddie. What do you think is at the root of her fear? Is there an antidote?

7. Paul believed in the "wildly persistent quality of human life." Why do you think God designed us to cling to life with such determination?

8. Paul desperately wanted to believe his brother would stay sober. What choices did he make about his brother's illness? What would you have done differently?

9. What do you think is the real root of Maddie's fear of the dark?

10. Bruce Lambert is described as relentless, but Maddie feels he has good motives for his actions. What are your impressions of Maddie's father?

11. Paul's brother, Mark, fights a battle against addiction. How does addiction touch the lives of other family members? What are the lasting impacts of loving someone with an addiction?

12. Paul is angry that God allowed the children to die in his care, yet he remains faithful. How can tragedy pull some closer to God and drive others further away?

13. Maddie is saddened that the tragedy eclipses all the good memories she made with Paul. How can she allow herself to remember past joys without letting them be eclipsed by sorrow?

14. What do you think the future holds for Katie Lambert?

15. Bruce Lambert clings tightly to his beliefs. How will he change when Paul reenters Maddie's life?

Love Inspired®
SUSPENSE

TITLES AVAILABLE NEXT MONTH

Available March 8, 2011

MISSION: OUT OF CONTROL
Missions of Mercy
Susan May Warren

FACE OF DANGER
Texas Ranger Justice
Valerie Hansen

CODE OF JUSTICE
Liz Johnson

DOUBLE IDENTITY
Diane Burke

REQUEST YOUR FREE BOOKS!

2 FREE RIVETING INSPIRATIONAL NOVELS
PLUS 2 FREE MYSTERY GIFTS

Love Inspired®
SUSPENSE

YES! Please send me 2 FREE Love Inspired® Suspense novels and my 2 FREE mystery gifts (gifts are worth about $10). After receiving them, if I don't wish to receive any more books, I can return the shipping statement marked "cancel". If I don't cancel, I will receive 4 brand-new novels every month and be billed just $4.24 per book in the U.S. or $4.74 per book in Canada. That's a saving of at least 23% off the cover price. It's quite a bargain! Shipping and handling is just 50¢ per book in the U.S. and 75¢ per book in Canada.* I understand that accepting the 2 free books and gifts places me under no obligation to buy anything. I can always return a shipment and cancel at any time. Even if I never buy another book, the two free books and gifts are mine to keep forever.

123/323 IDN FDCT

Name	(PLEASE PRINT)	
Address		Apt. #
City	State/Prov.	Zip/Postal Code

Signature (if under 18, a parent or guardian must sign)

Mail to the **Reader Service:**
IN U.S.A.: P.O. Box 1867, Buffalo, NY 14240-1867
IN CANADA: P.O. Box 609, Fort Erie, Ontario L2A 5X3

Not valid for current subscribers to Love Inspired Suspense books.

**Are you a subscriber to Love Inspired Suspense
and want to receive the larger-print edition?
Call 1-800-873-8635 or visit www.ReaderService.com.**

* Terms and prices subject to change without notice. Prices do not include applicable taxes. Sales tax applicable in N.Y. Canadian residents will be charged applicable taxes. Offer not valid in Quebec. This offer is limited to one order per household. All orders subject to credit approval. Credit or debit balances in a customer's account(s) may be offset by any other outstanding balance owed by or to the customer. Please allow 4 to 6 weeks for delivery. Offer available while quantities last.

Your Privacy—The Reader Service is committed to protecting your privacy. Our Privacy Policy is available online at www.ReaderService.com or upon request from the Reader Service.

We make a portion of our mailing list available to reputable third parties that offer products we believe may interest you. If you prefer that we not exchange your name with third parties, or if you wish to clarify or modify your communication preferences, please visit us at www.ReaderService.com/consumerschoice or write to us at Reader Service Preference Service, P.O. Box 9062, Buffalo, NY 14269. Include your complete name and address.

Conor Russell knows what prairie living can do to a delicate female—that's why he's raising his daughter, Rachael, to be tough. But can the new schoolteacher, Virnie, look beyond his hard exterior and help both Conor and his daughter experience a family once and for all?

Find out in PRAIRIE COWBOY by Linda Ford, available March 2011 from Love Inspired Historical.

"You wanted to speak to me?" Virnie kept her voice admirably calm despite the way her insides vibrated at speaking to Conor, who had inadvertently opened an unwelcome door in her heart.

Conor seemed very interested in the reins draped across his palm. "I have to go to Gabe's farm and help him with his harvest. Rae can't go with me."

"Of course not. She has to attend school."

Conor's gaze rested on Rachael standing near the school watching them. He loved her so much it seemed to almost hurt him.

"I will miss her." His voice was low, edged with roughness. "But out here we do what has to be done without complaining."

She nodded, not understanding the warning note in his voice any more than she understood why she ached inside.

He jerked his gaze away as if aware of the tension lacing the air between them. "She needs someone to stay with her. Would you?"

Her mouth fell open. Was this God's answer for a way to spend more time with Rachael? He'd certainly found a unique way of doing it.

"Why, I'd love to stay with her. On one condition. You allow me to teach her a few skills around the house."

They did silent battle with their eyes and then he nodded. "So long as you don't teach her to be a silly, weak female."

"Female doesn't necessarily equate with weak and silly." She'd tried to prove it to her father. She pushed the hurt of her former life back into the shadows. This was not about her. It was about Rachael.

"I have to leave immediately. Take good care of her." He waved Rachael over.

Virnie thought he looked as if he regretted it already. As she walked away she overheard him say, "Don't expect her to stay when things get hard."

Virnie grinned. If he thought she'd turn tail and run at the first challenge she encountered, he didn't know the things she'd faced in the past.

Don't miss PRAIRIE COWBOY by Linda Ford, available March 2011 from Love Inspired Historical.

Love Inspired®

With his Dreams Come True foundation, Ethan Fox turns wishes into reality. Now Ethan has come to care deeply for a sick boy whose dream is to have Ethan as a dad. After spending time with the sweet boy and his lovely mother, Lexie Carlson, Ethan wonders if this little boy's wish could come true after all.

A Dad of His Own
by
Gail Gaymer Martin

Available March 2011.

Dreams come True

Steeple Hill®

LI87657